praise for egghead

"… a sensitive examination of bullying and its psychological roots."
— *Booklist*

"The novel is satisfying and provocative, leaving readers with much food for thought. Hopefully more titles are on the horizon from this gifted writer."
— *The StarPhoenix (Saskatoon)*

"*Egghead* is a sensitive portrayal of the dynamics behind bullying, peer pressure, and search for identity."
— *The Bureau County Republican*

"The complicated boundaries of friendship are challenged and redefined in this story."
— *Today's Parent*

"The events of this novel are as poignant as they are deplorable, and students will likely see themselves or someone they know in each of the captivating characters. The novel is a quick and easy read and the format lends itself nicely to a character study as well as illustrating different features of text. The use of poetry and short, perspective-driven chapters make this an enjoyable and highly teachable resource."
— *Professionally Speaking*

"Egghead brings the lessons of bullying to life for kids. We try to teach them about compassion and empathy and the part of the iceberg that lies below the surface; however, nothing in my experience has highlighted the value of these lessons more effectively than this novel. I have taught it to classes at three different high schools, and to all types of students and the end result is always the same: the entire class is thoroughly engaged in the novel and they leave it with a renewed understanding of why people act the way they do. By getting inside the minds of a variety of characters, students are quick to make connections to their own lives and relate to the struggles and triumphs of all the characters in *Egghead*. This should be mandatory reading for all students navigating the complex social climate of Grade 9 today!"
—Jordan Burnie, Classroom teacher,
  Catholic District School Board of Eastern Ontario

"I have just finished reading *Egghead* to my Grade 8 English classes - they loved it! It was such a great opportunity learning about empathy and growth and change in characters. Many of the children could see themselves or others in various parts of the story. Thank you for tackling difficult subjects that are important for teens and young adults to think about and discuss in a safe environment. We will definitely be reading more of your work in the near future!"

— Karen Fleurie, Grade 8 teacher

Renfrew County District School Board

"I have 32 students, and I need to tell you that they couldn't put the book down … they loved it!"

— Nancy Fazari, Grade 7 teacher

Dufferin-Peel Catholic District School Board

"Thank you for writing the one book that has the ability to captivate my Grade 6 class. Several times throughout the day, someone will ask me to read some more. My students say they can identify with all the characters in the book and they appreciate how accurately you portray the struggle facing students at school. I know they want me to hurry up and finish reading *Egghead*, but when we're done they'll be wishing for more. Thanks again, *Egghead* was the perfect book to use to start the year!"

— Stacey Hillis, Grade 6 Teacher

Waterloo Region District School Board

"*Egghead* is my favorite book to use with Grade 7 students. *Egghead* addresses bullying from all sides, the bully, victim and bystander, and speaks to the struggle of each person involved! Beyond that, my students resonated with the character's at home struggles as well. There is something in this book for everyone!"
— Lauren Perkins
  Upper Canada District School Board

"Just finished reading *Egghead* to my new batch of Grade 8s and they, as most classes are, are blown away by its brilliance ... This book truly opens the minds of an age group of kids who are usually egocentric and lets them empathize, sympathize, and "feel" in ways that they hadn't before. Thank you once again for exciting kids with the best children's novel that I have ever come across."
— Chris Jackson, Grade 7/8 Teacher
  York Region District School Board

"My students and I loved reading *Egghead*. No matter the class or the year, it is a timeless story that students can relate to and learn from. It has become the story to which we compare other books of similar themes, and guides so much of our discussions of what it means to be compassionate, kind, and accepting. Middle school is tough, and we each have a little bit of Katie and Devan in us."
— Melissa Thompson, Teacher
  Ottawa Jewish Community School

"When I read *Egghead* to my Grade 7 students, you literally can hear a pin drop. We are all on the edge of our seats, waiting to see how each of the characters will react to the series of awkward, painful, devastating middle school events that are all too relatable. The novel also sparks wonderful discussion surrounding empathy towards others and our own role in being the bystanders."
— Tara Potter, Grade 7 Teacher
   Ottawa Catholic School Board

"... her characters allow the reader to follow along on their path as they find their way through bullying issues, and more importantly, make the powerful choices to be or not to be a bystander. I have read *Egghead* in the classroom for many years with my middle school students ... A poignant and important story of personal choices that delivers an important message and realities of acceptance and standing up for what is right, even if you are standing alone. All middle school students should read this book. A classic in the making ..."
— Chelsea Cleveland, Teacher
   Ottawa Jewish Community School

egghead Honors

- Chapters.ca Top 20 Bestselling Teens and Children's Books, 2008
- Kids Help Phone recommended resource
- YALSA "Sticks and Stones" selection
- One Book One School selection, Van Wyck, New York
- Red Maple Book Award - Fiction Honor Book 2009
- Snow Willow Award Nominee 2009
- CLA Young Adult Canadian Book Award shortlist, 2009
- Canadian Children's Book Centre Our Choice, 2009

other books by caroline pignat

Poetree, illustrated by François Thisdale

Shooter

The Gospel Truth

Unspeakable

Greener Grass

Wild Geese

Timber Wolf

EGGHEAD

A NOVEL

CAROLINE PIGNAT

Red Deer Press

EGGHEAD

A NOVEL

CAROLINE PIGNAT

Published in Canada by Red Deer Press,
195 Allstate Parkway, Markham, ON L3R 4T8

Published in the United States by Red Deer Press,
311 Washington Street, Brighton, MA 02135

Red Deer Press acknowledges with thanks the Canada Council for the Arts and the Ontario Arts Council for their support of our publishing program. We acknowledge the financial support of the Government of Canada through the Canada Book Fund (CBF) for our publishing activities.

 Canada Council   Conseil des arts
for the Arts   du Canada

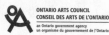 ONTARIO ARTS COUNCIL
CONSEIL DES ARTS DE L'ONTARIO
an Ontario government agency
un organisme du gouvernement de l'Ontario

Library and Archives Canada Cataloguing in Publication
Title: Egghead : a novel / Caroline Pignat.
Names: Pignat, Caroline, author.
Description: Anniversary edition.
Identifiers: Canadiana 20200153560 | ISBN 9780889955806 (softcover)
Classification: LCC PS8631.I4777 E44 2020 | DDC jC813/.6—dc23

Publisher Cataloging-in-Publication Data (U.S.)
Names: Pignat, Caroline, author.
Title: Egghead : a novel / Caroline Pignat.
Description: Markham, Ontario : Red Deer Press, 2020. | Originally published 2007. | Summary: "Together three young teens are struggling to find their way out of one of the classic dilemmas of life: how not to be a bystander to bullying, how to stand up for their friends, and how to deal with consuming rage" -- Provided by publisher.
Identifiers: ISBN 978-0-88995-580-6 (mass market)
Subjects: LCSH Bullying—Juvenile fiction. | Friendship—Juvenile fiction. | Anger in adolescence – Juvenile fiction. | BISAC: JUVENILE FICTION / Social Themes / Peer Pressure.
Classification: LCC PZ7.P546Egg |DDC [F] – dc23

Edited for the Press by Peter Carver
Cover design by Jacquie Morris
Text design by Erin Woodward

Printed in Canada By Houghton Boston

www.reddeerpress.com

for tony.

acknowledgements

Thanks so much to:

Peter Carver, my editor, for your expertise, guidance, and wonderful humor.

Marie Campbell, my agent. Thanks for your support and direction.

Authors Karleen Bradford and Rachna Gilmore. Thank you both for your inspiration and generous mentorship. I am so grateful for your instruction, encouragement, and advice.

Experts in the field: Barbara Coloroso, author of *The Bully, the Bullied and the Bystander*; Angela Lorusso-Stewart, Coordinator of the Bully Prevention Program and Sandra LeBlanc, Facilitator and Counsellor for the Confident Children's Program, both under the auspices of the Ottawa Community Resource Center; and Paramedic Kelly Edwards, for sharing your research and experience. You have all helped ensure that this novel rings true.

My crit girls Heather Burke, Christine Ferris, Sharon Rudnitski, and Elizabeth Tevlin for your insightful feedback. Donna, Lisa, and Karin for always being just an email away and to my "fans" in the hood. You've all been wonderful. I couldn't have asked for better travelling buddies along this writing journey.

A heartfelt thanks:

To my parents, Alan and Peggy Cranny, for teaching me to dream;

To my kids, Liam and Marion, for reminding me to play;

Especially to my husband, Tony. You have helped make so many of my dreams come true. Thanks for everything. I couldn't have done it without you.

Go to the ant, consider its ways, and be wise.
—King Solomon

william james reid

The First Day

Scurrying on the cold gym floor,
it stops,
antennae waving.

It will die in here.

One
cannot survive
alone.

It seeks its colony;
a place filled with others
just like it,

a place
where it belongs.

In quiet corners
it searches
for a scent

that isn't there.

Katie

The gym was packed that first day of grade nine. Among the crowd, I recognized our classmates from St. Anne's. Some looked different, others were trying to. As though new pants or a new hairstyle might help us believe we belonged here. But then I saw someone who was the same as ever.

Will.

"What's he doing?" Jenna asked, watching him creep along on his elbows and knees, nose to the floor and butt up in the air.

I shrugged. "Leave it to Will to find the one bug in a room of a hundred people." Not surprising, though. Will would choose bugs over people any day.

"For someone so smart, he sure acts stupid," Jenna said.

I couldn't argue with her, really. Will always did weird things like shoving raisins up his nose just to see how many would fit, or catching lice so he could "study their gestation." Last winter he even tested the lick-the-metal-fence theory. I still remember the tiny tongue-skin flag waving from the chain link. But that was just Will. We'd just shake our heads and get on with it. Like Granny always says, everyone's "different in one way or another." She was right too. After all, Jenna had allergies, Erin saw a social worker, Paulo's sister ran away from home . . . and my Dad had cancer.

Last year Mr. Donlan, our Grade 8 teacher, asked Jenna and me to be Will's partners at the science fair. We ended up doing ants. Actually, it was kind of neat. Our ant farm won first place. That's how I learned that even strange creatures I never knew anything about were pretty interesting after all.

Strange creatures, like ants and Will.

I watched him shuffle along on his knees and elbows, following whatever bug had found its way onto the gym floor. Jenna shook her head. "Sheesh! No wonder he doesn't have any friends."

"He's got us." I said.

"Whatever." She rolled her eyes and tugged my arm. "C'mon, let's go see if we're in the same homeroom."

Maybe it was because he was so weird. Or maybe no one really cared. But Will usually kept to himself. He liked being ignored, like a bug on a wall. Sure, some kids liked to catch bugs and pull their legs off one by one just for fun. But luckily for Will, none of us were like that.

Not yet.

"*Martina!*" A shout echoed around the gym. The short guy beside me cringed as the crowd parted like the Red Sea for three guys. The entire gym went silent.

"M-my name's M-M-Martin, Shane," the short guy said, clutching his schoolbag.

"Oh, excu-u-u-use me." Shane got right up in Martin's face. "Still a total loser, eh, Ma-ma-ma-martina? Some things never change."

"Still a loser," the tallest of the three echoed.

"Hey." Shane grabbed the leather schoolbag hanging on a long strap across Martin's chest. "Nice purse, Martina. You don't mind if I do a little back-to-school shopping, do ya?" Shane pulled the strap until it tightened across Martin's chest.

From the look of Shane, back-to-school shopping was not his thing. His ratty jeans and dingy T-shirt looked like they'd been worn all summer. Even his sneakers had holes.

Martin shook his head, standing as far away as the strap would allow, his eyes full of tears. Shane rummaged in the bag, pocketing whatever he wanted. "So," he sniffed the brown paper bag. "What's for lunch today, Martina?"

"T-t-tuna."

"T-t-tuna?! You know I hate t-t-tuna!" Shane dumped the lunch on the floor and watched the apple roll to a stop by Will, still hunched in the corner.

Shane's eyes lit up at the sight of Will. "What do we got here?" He nodded for his buddies to follow.

My stomach sank.

Devan

Shane's hilarious. I swear to God.

Like this one time, me and him were out sitting on the curb by the 7-11 with our Slurpies when some wicked huge fat kid pulls up on his bike. The guy's *totally* dripping sweat. He's huffing and puffing as he waddles by. And Shane goes, "Hey Dev, do you smell bacon?"

Holy crap. I laughed so hard Slurpie came out my nose. Talk about brain freeze. Then Shane followed the guy around the store, snorting and grunting like a pig. Man, I nearly wet my pants laughing. But that's Shane for you. He cracks everyone up.

Well, maybe not the fat kid.

So it's the first day of school, right? I go in the gym and everyone's checking everyone out. *Geek. Freak. Jock. Flirt. Nerd.* The guy ahead of me is wearing new jeans and white sneakers. *Loser.* Probably still got the tags sewn in the back. I got my mom to wash mine the week before. No way I want to look like a total tool.

The place was packed with new kids—even I felt kind of nervous, but then I see Shane.

"Hey," he says. "Nice lid." I pat down my hair, mad that I let Mom talk me into that haircut. "Is that gel? It is, isn't it? Hey, Brad, check out Spike here."

"Shut up." I shove him into the crowd. Good old Shane. Grade 9 just wouldn't be the same without him.

Shane goofs around with Martin and then, elbowing me, nods at some guy in the corner. A real winner. The weirdo is kneeling on all fours looking at a bug or something. I couldn't tell really, not before Shane's sneaker squashes it flat.

The guy looks up, mouth hanging open. He's in total shock. I can't see Shane smiling, but I know he is.

"Do you have any idea what you have done?" the guy yells, jumping to his feet. He sounds like my whiny kid sister and his face is getting red.

"Yeah," Shane goes, "I do."

"That was a mature female, full of eggs." The guy's voice is getting louder and higher with every word. "You just wiped out a . . . a . . . a whole generation!"

"Geez," Shane finally says to me over his shoulder. "You'd think I squashed *his* mother." Shane swipes his foot along the floor leaving a black smear. The guy starts shak-ing like he's going to explode or something.

"You got something to say, *Egghead*?" Shane asks.

"Yeah, Egghead, you wanna say something?" Brad echoes.

And just when it's about to get interesting, this girl comes out of nowhere and yells, "I do!"

Katie

Next thing I knew, there I was, right between Shane and Will. They both looked at me like *I* was the one acting crazy.

"Umm, I . . . uh . . ." I racked my brain for something, anything, to say. "That's bad luck, squashing a bug like that." Lame, I know, but what do you expect? I was under a lot of pressure.

"I thought," one of Shane's friends said, looking more confused than before, "it means your mother's gonna hurt her back."

The taller one shoved him. "That's step on a crack, Brad, ya loser!"

"Oh."

"Killing a bug means it's gonna rain."

Shane spun around. "Would you two shut up?" He turned back to me, even more furious. This diversion was not part of his plan, if you could call "find a dweeb—kick his butt" a plan. His dark eyes burned in their sockets. His fists clenched.

My heart pounded in my throat. I took a step back. Just a little one. Hardly noticeable to anyone else. But somehow, that couple of inches told Shane all he needed to know. His mouth slithered into a cold smile. The bell rang. But I knew it wasn't over.

In fact, it was just beginning.

william james reid

The Rope

The other boys
make it look so easy.
Hand over hand over hand
to the top.
Physics, really, I tell myself.
But I am stuck on the knot.

The rope
burns
my palms.
Tears
burn
my eyes,
as heckles echo

in the gym
and in my head.

Loser. Idiot. Spaz.

Slowly, but surely,
I slip
and dangle
at the
end
of
my
rope.

I will never understand
why we climb the rope.
What does it teach us, really,

except what we don't want to know.

Devan

Turns out William Reid is in our gym class. Which is great. Not that we want him on our team or nothing, but he'll be a fun opponent.

Gym is my favorite subject, but I admit I'm not too crazy about stripping down with thirty guys. It's just weird. My family's pretty private. Even Shane, who shares a room with his two younger brothers, tried to get out of changing. He told Panetta that there was no law saying he had to wear those purple shorts and gym shirt. In fact, he even said there should be a law against it.

He did eventually change into his gym stuff. But, typical Shane, he did it on his terms, coming out of the change room ten minutes late. Me and Brad had already climbed the rope three times each by then. It would have been more if we weren't waiting for Egghead. What a loser. I don't think he even got off the knot.

After booting it round the gym on that last lap, Shane is the first one in the change room after class. Man, he can run. By the time the rest of us start changing, he's already half dressed, reaching for his shirt.

But not before I see the bruise.

It spreads in a dark purple stripe across his back. Whatever hit him, hit him hard. The yellowed mark below it tells me it hit him often, too. My stomach sinks. Man, that's gotta hurt. I feel bad for him . . .

Shane catches me staring. "What the hell are you looking at?" He glares at me, daring me to answer him as he yanks his shirt on, then looks behind, making sure nobody else saw. But they didn't. They were too busy laughing at Egghead's underpants.

Egghead is standing there completely naked, except for his black socks and pink underpants. Yeah, I said pink. Can you believe it? It was guy's underwear all right, only I'd never seen ones that color before. The only thing pinker is his face. He's scrambling, trying to get dressed. But it's too late. All he manages to put on is his undershirt —only it isn't an undershirt really, just the neck part of his turtleneck or something. What a freak.

Egghead starts backing away from everyone. I dunno where he's going. He probably doesn't either, since now all his stuff is still on the other side of the room. Me and Brad step up behind Shane and Egghead's eyes go all huge. He's shaking, all twitchy and terrified like my sister's bunny, Lulu. It bit me the last time I tried to hold it. Stupid rabbit. Just 'cause I *could* wring its neck doesn't mean I would.

Anyways, I don't know what Egghead's problem is. We aren't even touching him.

"What's with the pink underwear?" Brad asks.

Egghead crosses his hands in front of his crotch, and mumbles something about the wash.

"Sounds to me like your mom needs a lesson in laundry," I say.

"Yeah," goes Brad. "Is she dumb or something?"

Well, that's it. Egghead cracks. He just starts screaming and freaking out.

But Shane's ready. "Open the door!"

Martin pulls it open, probably glad it wasn't him for a change. Egghead's so into his fit, he doesn't even notice Shane shove him into the hall. We close the door and lean our shoulders on it, holding it shut.

Egghead screams full throttle for a few more seconds. Then a girl yells.

"Oh man, the girls are coming out," someone beside me whispers.

Katie

I could not believe Will. *Streaking!* What was he thinking? Thank God I was the only one out of the girls' change room.

There he was, out in the hall in his underwear. His *underwear!* Well, his socks and his turtleneck dickie, too—as if those covered anything. I'd always thought wearing a dickie was a strange fashion choice, even for Will. He usually wore it tucked under his sweater collar to make it look like he wore a turtleneck. Odd, I know. But now, flapping around his bare collarbones as he jumped and yelled, the thing looked completely ridiculous.

"*Will!*" I shouted. But he didn't hear me. He was so into his fit, he didn't even know where he was. Or what he *wasn't* wearing. Will hadn't had a tantrum like this in a long time. He was always an emotional guy. Usually, if he was freaking out we'd just ignore him or leave him for a while. I thought about letting him be as I watched him whine, mutter, and hit himself in the head.

No. The girls would be coming out any minute. I couldn't leave him. Not like that.

"William, stop!" I snapped. "Stop it right now!"

He slowly opened his eyes, looking like he'd just woken up from a bad dream. Only it wasn't a dream. He *was* standing at school in his underwear. His mouth dropped as reality hit, then he screamed and ran for the boys' change room door, slamming into it with a thud. The door wouldn't budge.

Great, just great, I thought. He kept pushing against the door, his socks slipping on the marble floor. "It's locked!" I finally yelled.

He looked at me in total panic, then took off running down the hall. Clutching my gym uniform, I ran after him, hoping, *praying* that I'd find him before everyone else did. The bell would be ringing any minute.

He stood at his locker in his black socks, white turtle-neck dickie, and pink underwear, fumbling with the lock and muttering the combination like a mantra. "Fourteen–forty-five–twenty-two–fourteen–forty-five–twenty-two . . ."

I shoved my gym stuff at him. "Here, put this on! Hurry! The bell is—"

RRRIIINNG!

The doors swung opened and crowds spilled into the hall. Laughter rushed at us like a tidal wave. Clutching my gym clothes, Will hid behind me, exposing both of us.

"That's enough now, that's enough. Don't you people have somewhere to be?" Mr. Spence pushed his way through the crowd. For a principal, he was pretty short, smaller than most of the students. I'd have mistaken him for one if it weren't for his bald head and mustache. He waded through the crowd, stopping in surprise when he saw Will. "What . . . what's going on here?"

Will stood knock-kneed and red faced, desperately trying to cover his crotch with my gym shirt. It didn't work. He opened his mouth to answer Mr. Spence, but nothing came out.

Mr. Spence looked at me. I had no idea what to say. He sighed. "Put on your shorts and, both of you, follow me to the office. The rest of you, get to class."

Will trembled, stepping one leg and then the other into the shorts. I looked away, trying to give him his privacy, but the lingering crowd wasn't helping any. They giggled and laughed, heckled and joked. Shane came around the corner and joined in. He elbowed his buddy. The two of them were killing themselves laughing.

Eager to get out of the hall, I started to follow Mr. Spence, but Will didn't move. His hips looked shrink-wrapped in my tiny shorts as he stood against the lockers, hands still crossed in front of him. A dark stain spread across the shorts and I noticed the puddle of yellow on the marble floor by his locker.

"Come on, Will." I said, pulling his arm until he staggered forward.

"Mop to aisle two . . . mop to aisle two!" Shane called from the crowd and they all laughed.

william james reid

One Red Sock

White underwear
turns pink
when washed with
one red sock.

Change rooms have no stalls,
to hide the underwear
turned pink from
one red sock.

People stop,
stare,
and laugh,
at the sight

of underwear washed with
one red sock.

Something
lets
go
and
runs
down
my leg
into
a puddle of hot embarrassment.

All because of
one red sock.

Devan

"Holy crap! Did you see that?" the crowd says.

"I know. He peed right there. In front of everyone," it answers. More laughter. "What's with his mother?" it asks as we climb the stairs to next class.

"Didn't you know?" goes Paulo DiPalma, some kid from Egghead's old school. "She's dead."

It echoes in the stairwell.

Dead.

Dead.

Dead.

I feel bad. I mean, I wouldn't have mentioned her if I'd known that.

No wonder he freaked out. But how was I supposed to know? He could've told us. I mean, he should've said something, instead of just acting like a total weirdo, right?

"What's with that *girl* who's always trying to save Egghead?" Shane says. "That was her, wasn't it, in the hall?"

"Yeah."

"Serves them right." Shane smiles. He looks pleased with how things are turning out. "Freakin' weirdos."

I didn't think she seemed all that weird. Other than the fact that she thought she could stand up to Shane. I have to admit, for such a cute little thing, she's got guts.

Did I say she was cute? Well, I mean cute, like, small cute. Like how kittens are cute. Oh, never mind.

I just wonder when I'll see her again. And what Shane's going to do when *he* does.

Katie

My stomach twisted as I followed Mr. Spence into his office. I couldn't believe I was here. Me, Katie McGillvary, straight-A student and all-around rule follower. What would Dad think? I hoped he wouldn't have to know. He wasn't feeling all that great these days, what with the chemo and all. The last thing I wanted was to stress him out with something like this.

Mr. Spence motioned for me to sit in the chair. He eyed Will, and placed a plastic grocery bag on the other chair's cushion. I don't know how he managed in those tight, wet shorts, but somehow Will sat.

"Now, Will, your clothes are . . ."

Will shrugged. Mr. Spence had taken us by the change rooms on the way to the office, but Will's clothes were long gone.

"Do you have any explanation for this?" Mr. Spence asked. Again, Will shrugged.

Mr. Spence looked at me. I told him what I'd seen. He stroked his mustache as he listened, then nodded and turned his attention back to Will. "Son, I need to know who is responsible. I can't help unless you help me help you." He paused. "Why were you in the hallway in your underwear? Is anyone harassing you?"

Will stared at the carpet.

Finally, Mr. Spence typed something in his computer and picked up the phone. "Well, I suppose the least I can do is get you some clothes . . . yes, hello, Professor Reid? Principal Spence here . . . there has been an incident . . ."

Will slumped lower in his chair at the sound of his father's name. I'd never met Professor Reid before. He never came to any school events, even when Will, Jenna, and I won last year's science fair. I guess professors were too busy. He sure wouldn't appreciate having to come because his son lost his pants and wet his shorts.

"Yes. Thank you, Professor. I look forward to meeting you." Mr. Spence hung up and checked his watch. "He should be here in ten minutes. You are free to go back to class now," he said to me as he walked around his desk.

"Would it be okay, sir, if I stayed with Will for a while . . . until his father comes?"

Mr. Spence glanced at Will trembling in the chair. Despite the little he had on, I doubted it was from the cold. "Sure. I've got hall duty but I'll be back shortly." He closed the door behind him.

We sat in silence for a while. Finally I spoke. "What really happened?"

"The boys." Will's voice was soft and shaky. "They . . . I dunno . . . I was trying to get dressed and . . ."

"What boys?"

"Sh-shane and his friends. Everybody."

"Why didn't you tell Mr. Spence, Will? He can't help you if you don't tell him."

Will looked at me then, his eyes teary. "And what do you think they would do to me, Katie? Huh? Getting them in trouble wouldn't help anyone, least of all me." He looked away and wiped his cheek. "If I don't say anything, it ends here."

I wanted it to be true, for his sake. Maybe both of us hoping might make it true. We sat without speaking until a knock came at the door.

"Mr. Spence?"

Will jumped to his feet at the sound of the voice. I opened the door. The man on the other side *had* to be Will's dad. It was like seeing the Will of the future. Same hair parted just above the left ear, same cords, V-neck sweater and turtleneck—although his was probably a full turtleneck and not just the neck part, the dickie that Will always wore. His eyes swept past me.

"William James Reid! What in the name—"

"Sorry, Dad—it was an accident. I . . . I'm sorry."

"Here." His father frowned and handed him a bag. "Put these on. You can't be running around the school in . . . in that!" He didn't seem to care what had happened. All that mattered was having the right appearance.

"I'll see you later, Will." I said.

"Sorry about your shorts, Katie," he answered, eyes down.

I was about to tell him not to worry, that I had a spare pair, but Professor Reid cut in. "*Her* shorts? Why in God's name are you wearing her shorts?"

I clicked the door behind me. The least I could do was let Will have that moment in private.

I joined my English class in the library.

"I still can't believe Will did that," Jenna whispered, sliding in the seat beside me. "I mean, he's weird and all that, but I didn't think he was like *streaker* weird."

"It was an accident." I argued. "He didn't do it on purpose."

"I heard he wears ladies underwear. Is that true?" she asked, eyes wide. "Did you, like, see *everything*?"

"I—"

"No, wait," she stuck her fingers in her ears. "Don't tell me. I don't want to know."

If Will thought being caught in the hall in pink underwear was the most devastating thing that could happen to him, he definitely wasn't prepared for the aftershocks. The story had a life of its own. By the end of that period, most of St. Patrick's High School was convinced Will Reid wore a pink thong and garters under his brown cords. Will was famous now, for all the wrong reasons.

And thanks to Will, I was too.

william james ʀeid

Teacher's Manual

Mr. Donlan knew
About me,
About Mom,
About my ways.

Mr. Donlan knew a lot.

But I wonder
if he knew
high school teachers wouldn't know.

And there is
no teacher's manual
on me.

Devan

The underwear dangles from the lock. It's pink, just like all the other ones.

Egghead comes out of class. You can see him freeze up when he notices what's hanging from his lock again. He pulls his ruler from his book and tries to jimmy them off, but when he flicks his wrist, the panties go flying through the air and land right in front of Spence who just happens to be patrolling the hall. Stopping, Spence picks them up and turns to Egghead.

"Yours?" Spence asks, holding them out.

Egghead shakes his head, no.

"I think we need to talk about this. Maybe discuss some strategies," Spence says, pocketing the panties and walking Egghead down the hall.

"Where are you getting all the panties?" I ask Shane. Pretty much every day for the past week there's been a pink pair on Egghead's locker, all different sizes and shapes. One time there was even a pair of those wicked-huge gramma underpants and another time there was a matching bra.

"How do I know?" he goes. "I just brought the first pair."

Leave it to Shane to start a new tradition.

Egghead may not think it's funny. I bet there's a few older sisters missing some underwear who don't think it's funny either. But I think it's hilarious.

We get our stuff and head to class. "Hey," Shane elbows me. "I wonder what'll happen to Spence when Mrs. Spence finds those in his coat pocket." We crack up all over again.

"See ya after class," Shane says, going into Peloso's room. I head up the stairs, still laughing as I round the corner and slam into someone.

Only it isn't just someone.

It's her.

She falls back on her butt from the impact. Even her glasses get knocked off. Papers float down around her and all over the floor.

"Oh, sorry," I say, getting her glasses and giving her a hand up. She stands, a little wobbly, and puts her glasses on. They sit all cockeyed on her face as she looks at me kind of dazed.

"Are you okay?" I ask. I must've hit her harder than I thought.

We both notice that I'm still holding her hand. My face burns and I let go real quick and bend down to pick up her papers. Drawings actually.

"Hey, these are really good," I say, stopping to look at them one by one.

"They're of Brayside," she says, still stunned. "My Granny's farm. I love it there."

Her drawings were fantastic. A cat. A man on a dock. But the best one was her. I couldn't stop looking at it.

She—I mean, it was beautiful.

Katie

They were the sketches from Brayside; Gizmo stretched out in a sunbeam licking his paws, the birches by the creek. Dad sitting on the dock dangling his feet in the lake. That one was my favorite. I couldn't wait to finish it—somehow, my pencil had captured the moment. It was so *Dad*. Granny said that old dock was always his favorite place, even as a little boy. He had his face turned up to the sun and you couldn't really see it, but you just knew he was smiling.

Devan stopped at the last drawing, my self-portrait. Mr. Cameron said to use a reference photo that was "emotionally charged, one that moves you," so I picked the one of me sitting on Granny's log fence singing the theme song from *Titanic* (my favorite movie). Thanks to my singing, and Granny saying I sounded like Gizmo in heat, Dad couldn't stop laughing. I don't know how he took the picture in focus. I hadn't heard him laugh like that in a long time. The chemo left him so drained. Gray like the ashes from the cigarettes he used to smoke. Some days he looked older than Granny.

But that day—that day was a good one.

Devan looked at that drawing, a *long* time. It felt weird to have Devan, *Shane's* Devan, looking at my sketches. Especially that one of me.

I looked at it in his hands: me, straddling the fence, arms up and chest out like I was flying. What a stupid grin. And look at my hair, uncut, uncombed, a rat's nest of tangles and straw. I looked like a total idiot.

In all the time I'd been working on the piece, studying every detail, somehow I had never noticed the big picture of how *dumb* I looked, like some scrawny, freckled scarecrow with dirty bare feet. Why hadn't I just drawn my class picture like everyone else? Maybe then I wouldn't have felt so . . . exposed. Like Devan was seeing something he shouldn't.

My face grew hotter the longer he stared. I shifted from foot to foot. Finally, I held out my hand.

"Not bad," he said, passing it back and laughing. "But it needs work. Things look a bit . . . flat."

I couldn't believe it. *Flat?*

My jaw dropped for a moment as the insult sank in. Not that it was news to me. I already knew I wasn't big-boob gorgeous like the senior girls. I didn't need Jenna's dumb *Sixteen Magazine* quiz to tell me that. I didn't need to hear the lingerie lady at the mall say, "Sorry dear, bras don't come any smaller." I didn't have to do the math to know 27-25-27 didn't add up to a great figure. And I certainly didn't need Devan Mitchell to tell *me* my body "needed work."

I snatched the sketch out of his hand. He looked stunned. *He must be stupider than I thought. He doesn't even know what he said wrong.*

"You're such a . . . a . . ." I looked him over, trying to find a great comeback. " . . . a goof!" I blurted. It was the first insult I could think of. Too bad it was so pathetic.

I saw the laughter in his eyes and, not waiting around to hear it, I ran all the way to class. My head swam with questions.

Why did God make boys so stupid?

Why did God make me so flat?

Why do I even care what Devan thinks?

And why, I thought as I entered the classroom, *am I crying?*

Devan

That's her name. Katie.

I think she hates me.

Probably because I knocked her down. God, I'm such an idiot. First I clock her in the hall, and then I start giving her an art critique. As if someone who can draw as well as her needs advice from me. I just thought the fence's perspective was off. The vanishing points were all wrong. I was trying to impress her. I should've just kept my big mouth shut. Dad's the architect, not me. I may have visited his studio a couple of times, but seriously, what do I know? Not much about art. Even less about girls.

She's right. I really am a goof.

Shane and Brad don't take advanced science, but Dad made me take it. But I'm glad I'm in it now. It's the only class I have with Katie. Something about her being there makes it better. Even when I'm sitting through Jackson's lectures. Man, that guy can talk! Last week we sat through his twenty-minute speech on what we'll find inside a worm. Yeah, worm guts. Duh!

But the good news is that I ended up in Katie's group, with Egghead and some girl called Erin. We've been working together on this worm project for the last few classes. Which gives me some chances to make up for whatever I did to upset her. Only I don't know what to say.

Jackson finally shuts up and passes out the worms. "Ewww." Erin starts griping the moment Egghead pulls ours out of the jar. "That is like so disgusting."

It does smell bad, even for a dead worm. Must be the formaldehyde. Although pretty much any dead thing I've seen reeked.

One time last year, Shane found a dead rat somewhere and we stuck it in Kronke's desk—the drawer where she kept treats, the one she hardly ever opened. Anyways, it stayed there for three days of a June heat wave. By the time Kronke found it, it smelled so strong it burned. Kinda like tar mixed with egg and fart. The janitor lifted it out of the drawer by the tail. All the girls screamed. The freakin' thing moved! I swear. Then the fur bust open and out came these little wriggling maggots. Sarah Crawford puked right there.

Now *that* was gross. But this, this is just a plain, old, dumb worm.

Katie and Egghead are wearing their goggles and gloves. They lay the worm on the dissection tray, like they're prepping for the O.R.

Egghead holds out his hand. "Scalpel."

Katie hands it to him.

"Pin."

Katie's got it in her fingers, like they read each other's minds or something. He takes the pin, then four others, and spreads the worm like a hot dog bun. Katie leans in and pushes some of the greasy guts around with the forceps. She hooks a stringy thing.

"Oh. My. God." Erin goes. "Totally dis-gusting."

"Ah," Egghead says. "The dorsal blood vessel."

"So, uh . . . Katie," I go, standing there with my hands in my pockets. "How did Cameron like your drawings?"

She freezes and gives me this look. Man, she really hates me. But I can't stop myself. "I'm doing animation for the science fair."

"Uh-huh," she says, going back to the worm. "Here, Will, the crop and gizzard."

"You mean like *cartoons*?" Erin asks, as if I said I was studying *Sesame Street*. I turn my shoulder to block her out.

Katie pokes the worm with a pin. Something green squirts on my shirt. I pretend not to notice, but man, it's hard to be cool with worm snot on you.

"Umm . . . Jackson said we could do it in partners? You know? Uh . . . if we wanted to?" Everything is coming out like a question. Only I haven't even gotten to that yet. I sound like a total loser. Erin gags in the background.

"Partners are good," Katie says removing something like a spaghetti noodle and laying it on the tray, "if you don't get stuck doing all the work. Intestine."

She likes the idea of partners. Good. I take a deep breath.

"So I was just wondering, you know, if you like drawing and animation and that—"

"Will," she interrupts, "check this out. I think I found the aortic arches!"

"—maybe we could, you know . . ." I keep rambling, as Will pushes me aside for a better look.

"Totally gross!" Erin groans, watching them slide something into the dish.

Will looks at Katie's discovery with a magnifying glass. "You're right, they are, and you've removed all five intact!"

Katie smiles. Jackson comes over and gets just as excited. *What's the big deal? We see worm guts all over the street every time it rains. Big woop.*

"Well done, group three." Jackson smiles at us over his clipboard and writes something down. "Be sure to include that in your report."

Will goes back to his diagrams. Erin's rolling the intestine between her fingers like a mini play dough snake. And Katie looks up as if noticing me there for the first time.

"Did you say something, Devan?" she asks. My face gets hot. I'd never heard her say my name before. It sounds nice.

"I . . . uh," I look away and mumble. "Well, it's just that I . . . uh . . . I thought maybe you might—do you want to be my partner for the science fair?"

It rushes out in one breath but, right away, I want it back. I know the answer by the look on her face.

"No," she says. Just like that.

She's looking at me like *I'm* an experiment standing there with my heart gutted. Just like that worm, only less interesting to her.

Egghead comes over with his woop-de-doo diagrams. "Here's my contribution. Our report is almost complete."

Geek.

Katie puts them in the folder behind her outline and Erin's introduction. Then all three look at me, like they're waiting for something.

"Look, Katie," I blurt. "I'm sorry about knocking you over and all, I just think you're real artistic, and I know if you just give me a chance we could really be an awesome team . . . uh . . . for the science fair, I mean."

"Will's my partner," she says.

Erin pinches the intestine until worm turds come out.

I just want to disappear. God, I feel like such an idiot for asking her. Things couldn't get worse.

Then Erin turns and barfs all over my new shoes.

Katie

He'd asked me to be his partner for the science fair and, for a second, I thought he was serious. I mean, he said I was artistic and everything. But come on. Devan? *Shane's* Devan?

He probably asked me so I'd do the project for him. Just like how I have to write the worm report conclusion he totally "forgot" about. Or maybe it was just a big joke to ask the geeky girl. Devan Mitchell could have any girl he wanted in the school. Well, ninth grade at least. Shane probably put him up to it.

Devan left to wash his shoes and never came back. Erin was at the nurse's. So it was up to Will and me to clean up after our group. Typical. After everything was cleared away I told Will I just had to run to the washroom. I left the lab and headed down the hall.

Shane sat against the lockers outside Mr. Peloso's room—he was probably kicked out. He glared at me and stood. I looked the other way as I walked past, my stomach in knots. His sneakers squeaked behind, following me down the empty hall. My heart pounded as my imagination raced. *What's he doing? Why's he following me?*

It took everything I had not to run. I didn't want him to know he was getting to me, but he was. I turned into the girls' washroom and quickly locked the door behind me, unsure if I wanted to pee or throw up. I rinsed my face in cold water and waited. The bell was going to ring any second. I figured it would be safer to go back out in a crowd.

Will and I had been doing our best to avoid Shane the past few weeks. It was one of the "strategies" Will said Mr. Spence gave him. But they weren't working out all that well.

1. *Report all incidents.*

But Will refused to say anything or name names.

2. *Avoid the antagonist.*

That never worked. Shane seemed to seek Will out.

3. *Talk to your parents.*

As if! I couldn't see Will sharing any of this with his dad.

4. *Stay with a group.*

Didn't Mr. Spence see? All Will had was me and what help was I?

5. *Use humor.*

Right. Humor wasn't one of Will's strong points.

6. *Use positive self-talk.*

I knew Will used this one. Or tried to, at least. I heard his voice in the empty hall yesterday afternoon. "I am a good person. I am smart. People like me."

Mr. Spence told Will the teachers were informed and would be looking out for him, but I didn't see any of that either. I don't think our new teachers knew much about any of us. With so many grades and classes to teach, I was surprised they even knew our names. I missed Mr. Donlan's gold stars. I missed staying in to cut bubble letters for his bulletin boards. I even missed his corny titles like *Measurement Rules* or *Geology Rocks*.

Mr. Donlan knew us. He knew our families. It mattered to him whether or not we had done our homework, ate a good breakfast, or felt sad. Grade 9 teachers didn't care if we ran out without a hat, left projects till the night before, or ate all of our lunches. We were a few faceless kids out of hundreds. Names and numbers on a list. None of them, not one of my new teachers, ever asked how Dad was doing. Or me. I doubted they even knew Dad was sick. I guess they were just too busy.

The bell finally rang. I unlocked the door and joined the crowd in the hall. Shane was gone.

"Katie, you should see the tunnels they've made," Will said, as I entered the lab. "The nursery workers have been sorting and moving the young all week. They'll be hatching just in time."

Will picked up his books and headed for the door. "So, you're coming tonight, right? Wait till you see them in the new ant farm, Katie. They just love it." His enthusiasm was contagious.

"I think we'll place in the science fair," I said, not wanting to jinx it. I wanted so badly to win, to make Dad proud.

"*Place?*" Will said, and shook his head. "Who *else* has been working on a project since last year? Who *else* has three generations of ants? Who *else* is going to give the judges a front row seat to metamorphosis?" He held the door for me.

"So you think we'll place first?" I asked.

He smiled. "Who else?"

Devan

"No way." Shane says to me at lunch. "*No. Way.*" He laughs. "That, my friend, is friggin' disgusting."

"I know," I look at my wet shoes. "I'm gonna have to throw them out."

"Not the barf, loser," Shane says through a mouthful of chips. That was all he ever ate for lunch. Chips and a pop he ripped off some kid. "Egghead and Katie." He shakes his head. "Man, why any girl, even McGeek, would want to go out with that guy is beyond me."

"They aren't *going out*. They're just doing a science fair project together."

I never told Shane I got shot down or that I even asked her to be my partner. He wouldn't understand. So I give him the same explanation Katie gave me just before I left to clean up. "They incubated some larvae in Grade 8. I guess they're just extending on that project with the colony."

Shane's mouth drops open. He stares at me and then raises one eyebrow. *"Incubating larvae? Extending on a project with the colony?"* He's making air quotations as if those words aren't even English. ""Listen to *you,* brainiac." He rolls his eyes. "You don't even know what the hell you're talking about."

"Yeah." I laugh. It isn't funny, but I laugh just the same. Truth is, Shane doesn't know what the hell I am talking about.

"When's the science fair?" he asks. Something is brewing in the back of his mind.

"End of the month."

"Good," he says, emptying the crumbs in his mouth and wiping his chin. "That gives me a few weeks to come up with a plan, while *you* do our project." He stops to give some kid a wedgie. "What's it on, anyway?"

"Animation," I mumble, watching the kid head for the washroom, bowlegged and butt-numb, like he just got off a horse.

"Wicked." Shane says, slapping me on the back. "I love cartoons."

Katie

"Don't you see?" Jenna explained as we walked home. "You are *totally* acting like his girlfriend." She counted off the evidence on her fingers. "You are lab partners, you've seen him naked—"

"He *wasn't* naked," I interrupted. "He had on—"

"Well, whatever," she continued. "In his *underwear* then. You are partners for the science fair. You stood up to Shane for him. And now you're going on a *date*?"

"It's not a date. We're working on our project."

"Well, you never got invited to his house before."

"Mr. Donlan let us work on it at school last year." I said. I couldn't figure out why Jenna was making such a big deal of it. We'd even asked her to join us, but she said she was doing "The Telephone" with Isabella Montana, a girl she'd just met.

"Will is just a friend." I finally said. "Not even. He's more like my little brother."

"Well, duh!" Jenna rolled her eyes. "*I* know *you* don't like him that way. But the more time and attention you give that weirdo, the more other people are going to start thinking of you guys as a couple."

"*Part-ners*," I stressed, "not couple."

Jenna shrugged. "Once everyone believes it—well, it might as well be true." She stopped and looked me square in the eyes. "And I sure wouldn't want anyone saying that about any friend of mine." She headed up her driveway and didn't look back.

At first, I thought she was concerned about me, but as I walked on to Will's house, I realized what she was really saying. Jenna wouldn't be my friend if I was Will's.

I don't know what annoyed me more; that people cared about who I was or wasn't friends with, or that *I* cared what they cared.

I did the right thing helping Will, didn't I?

He knows we're just project partners, right?

My mind started spinning as I reached his street.

What if she is right? What if people started treating me like Will?

I didn't know what to think. But I did know that I'd hate to be labeled as Mrs. Egghead for the rest of my life. I kicked a crab apple off the path.

We never had these problems last year. Jenna and I were best friends. And Will was just . . . well . . . Will.

Why do things have to change?

I climbed the steps to the big stone house and rang the bell. Will was expecting me. Our eggs were hatching.

Only now I wasn't as excited about seeing them.

His dad answered. He gave me a strange look over his reading glasses, like *I* was the one who'd been running around the school in my underwear.

I shifted from foot to foot. "Uh . . . hi, Professor Reid."

"Will is in the solarium," he said and walked back down the hall. "I'll be in the study if you need me."

I didn't know what or where the solarium was, but I was not about to ask. I wandered down the hall. Their house was interesting. Not like anywhere you'd think a kid would live. But then again, this was Will's place, and he wasn't like any kid I knew.

The ticking of the grandfather clock echoed around the walls. It was the loudest clock I'd ever heard, or maybe it was just that their house was so quiet. I stopped to look at a family portrait over the fireplace. It was from a few years ago, before Mrs. Reid died. Will was never the same after the accident. My mother died when I was born. I never knew her, not in person anyway. *Maybe it's better that way,* I thought, remembering how Will still struggled with that grief. *Maybe it is better not to know what you are missing.*

"Hello, Katie."

I jumped at the sound of Will's voice. He seemed so happy to see me. Almost too happy.

Maybe this isn't such a good idea. Maybe Jenna is right.

"Your dad . . . um . . ." I stammered.

He knows we're partners, right? Like this isn't a date or anything.

I didn't know where to look. "Professor Reid . . . in the study . . ."

" . . . with the lead pipe," Will added, his blue eyes laughing. We'd often played *Clue* on rainy day recesses in

Mr. Donlan's class. "You think *that's* bad," Will said, scooping up a fat blonde cat. "I just found Colonel Mustard in the lavatory drinking from the bowl!"

We burst out laughing and I knew everything was going to be okay. Will was still Will. He hadn't changed.

We hadn't changed.

william james ʀeid

Ant Farm

They tunnel in darkness,
trusting
their path is right,
knowing
they will eventually
connect.

They create their world
one grain at a time.
So close,
and yet,
so unaware
that I am watching
and smiling.

It makes me wonder
if someone close to me
might be watching—
And smiling.

Devan

I knock on Shane's screen door and sit on the step. He's always late. If I didn't come pick him up, he'd probably never make the bus.

I didn't think much about Shane's "plans" for the science fair. I got enough to worry about, getting "our" project together. Luckily Dad has a friend who owns an animation studio. He took me on the weekend. I got a ton of neat stuff. Storyboards. Model sheets. Even a clip from the show. But I still have to work on the presentation. And the science fair is less than a week away.

Now I know what Katie meant about getting stuck with a partner where *you* do all the work. Egghead's a weirdo and all, but I bet he does his fair share.

"I don't have to listen to you! You're not my father!" Shane barges out and slams the screen door behind him. "C'mon," he yanks my arm. "Let's go."

Blood trickles from a cut at the corner of his mouth. He's hurrying me down the driveway just as the screen door explodes open. We start running.

"Yeah, you better run, you little bastard!" It's Riley, Shane's mom's boyfriend. His massive shoulders fill the entire door frame. "You'll be sorry. You good-for-nothing little—"

We don't hang around to hear the rest. Not that we haven't heard it all before.

Shave a bear and you'd get Riley. He moved in about a year ago, when Shane started missing school. I never asked him about it, but I knew. That's when I started seeing the bruises on his face and arms. Bruises from bear wrestling, if you know what I mean. I don't know what his mom sees in that guy. Neither does Shane. But we don't talk about it much.

All I *am* saying is that only a smart kid, a real smart kid, can survive the kind of life Shane is living. He might have failed Grade 8 once, but Shane is the smartest guy I know. Only those smarts aren't the kind teachers like.

We run around the corner and slow to a walk. "What's his problem?" I ask.

"The principal called." Shane picks up a rock and chucks it at the bus stop sign. "Wanted to 'discuss my behavior' with Riley. *Riley!* Can you believe it?"

"Why didn't Spence speak to your mom?" I ask.

Shane shrugs. "Riley wasn't saying much on the phone, just stuff like: '*Zero tolerance, I agree.*' His face got redder by the second. '*Oh, I'll talk to Shane, Mr. Spence. Don't worry about that,*' he goes staring me down across the room. Then as soon as the phone is down, he comes at me all fired up because I'd hurt some kid he doesn't even know."

"Who ratted you out—did he say?" It could have been anyone, really. It's only October and already every Grade 9 kid knows Shane Duran. Just yesterday, he pantsed Martin, stuck a pair of pink underwear on Egghead's locker, and tossed some other kid in the dumpster. All before third period. That kid deserved it, though. He stank. Take a freakin' shower, man!

Last week, I still don't know how, Shane even managed to get Paulo DiPalma to start a food fight. *Paulo.* The guy's own *mother* is a lunch monitor! Man, *she* sure wasn't happy. Got clocked square in the face with a fruit cup and dropped like a hockey bag. That's *got* to hurt. She even got two black eyes. Not that we ever saw her again. But I heard from Paulo. Way I see it, Shane did him a favor. Who wants their mom watching them hang at school, making sure they eat their sandwich crusts? No, thanks.

So, like I said, it really could have been anyone that ratted out Shane.

"It's Egghead," Shane says through clenched teeth. He's got that look in his eye. "I just know it," he mutters as the bus stopped in front of us. "He'll be sorry. Won't know what hit him. The good for nothing little—"

I don't wait to hear the rest. It sounds way too familiar.

The second we're off the bus, Shane makes a beeline for Egghead's locker.

Katie

Jenna checked her hair in my locker mirror while I piled books into my arms.

"Did you know Isabella is Mike Montana's sister?" She tried to sound surprised. As if she didn't know. She knew everything else about the guy—he wore number 22, he played senior boys basketball, his locker was on the third floor. Jenna had dog-eared every page in her sister's yearbook that had Mike's picture. Yet *amazingly* she had just discovered the love of her life had a sister, who *happened* to be her very own science fair partner.

What a coincidence.

For some crazy reason, maybe puberty, Jenna thought she had a chance of finding true love with a senior. Unlike her *Sixteen Magazine* heartthrobs, Mike was, after all, right here in the same building. I just didn't have the heart to tell her she'd have more luck getting a movie star to ask

her out. Even the makeup she'd just put on in the washroom didn't help. Jenna looked like what she was—what
we both were. Grade 9 tourists, totally lost in the world of
teenagers.

"I don't know why you even have a locker," Jenna said
as I heaved my stuff onto my hip and slammed the door
shut with my foot. "You carry everything." She showed me
her tiny, pink purse and matching clipboard. We both
knew five minutes into class she'd be asking me for a pen
and paper.

Neither of us had mentioned Will and I wasn't about
to bring it up. Whether she liked it or not, Will and I were
working on our project. But I did decide to avoid Will a
bit more at school, just in case. Just so no one would take
it the wrong way.

"I know it was you!" Shane's voice echoed in the hall
as he and Devan blew past me, stopping up ahead. Kids
gathered around, elbowing in for a ringside seat as Shane
shoved Will up against the lockers

"Come on," Jenna said, pulling me in the opposite
direction. "This doesn't have anything to do with us."

I let her lead me away, trying to convince myself that
Will could take care of himself.

Yeah, right.

That, if things went bad, somebody in that crowd
would do something to help.

As if.

That Will didn't know I was there, and wouldn't know
that I had abandoned him.

I abandoned him.

The truth of it hit me about as hard as he was hitting
the lockers.

Shane had him by the neck. "If you ever . . ." SLAM! "
. . . ever . . ." SLAM! " . . . *EVER* go crying to Spence again
it'll be the last thing you do!"

"I didn't . . . I didn't . . ." Will's words choked in his
throat as his face turned darker shades of red.

Everyone else just stood around watching. *Why was-
n't somebody stopping it?*

"Don't!" Jenna cried, but not at Shane. She grabbed
my wrist. My books fell to the floor as I pulled away.
"Katie, *don't!*" she pleaded, but I was already running back.

Somebody had to do something, even if that somebody was me.

william james reid

The Samurai Ant

The Samurai ant
is large
and strong.
Its mandibles are smooth,

perfect for fighting,

but not for digging,
carrying,
or building.

A Samurai ant
cannot even feed itself.

Its colony
would die
if it did not
enslave other ants.

They
are its source
of power,
strength,
and support.

Too bad the other ants
don't know.

Devan

"Leave him alone!" someone shouts from behind me.

It's Katie.

"Stay out of it," I say. I admired her standing up to Shane before. But today, today is different. Shane is different. He's not looking for fun; he wants revenge. Can't she see that? For someone so smart, she is acting pretty stupid.

Shane's so far gone, he doesn't even hear her. He's got a fistful of Egghead's turtleneck and he's twisting it something fierce. Egghead's face is turning purple. I can tell by the way Shane's other hand tightens that he's going to blow any second.

"Stop it! *Stop!* You're hurting him!" Katie yells, pushing past.

It all starts happening in slow motion. Shane hears someone come at him from behind. He turns. He cocks his arm and shoots out his fist like a cannonball.

I don't remember doing it, but I grab Katie and pull her back just in time to see Shane's punch swing inches by her face. I might've saved her life, or her glasses at least. But she doesn't even thank me. In fact, she starts freaking out.

"Let me go! *Let! Go!*" She's screaming and kicking my shins like some kind of maniac. I'm so surprised to be holding her, and to be on the receiving end of her self-defense moves, I forget to let go. At least until she gives me a killer blow to the ribs with her bony little elbow.

"Whoa," I throw my hands up in the air. "Easy!"

She jumps away from me like *I* was hurting *her*.

R-r-r-rip!

Egghead slides down the lockers to the floor, leaving Shane holding nothing but a scrap. Egghead's turtleneck.

"What the—" Shane says, looking from the scrap to Egghead. "What the hell are you wearing?"

The pasty color's coming back to Egghead's face as he slowly stands. "It's a dickie."

"A *what*?" Shane asks, his face not so red anymore either.

"A *dick-eeee*." Egghead grabs it from Shane and wraps it around his blotchy neck, tucking the bib back under his sweater. "A fake turtleneck."

Shane busts out laughing.

"A *dickie*? You're wearing a *dickie*? Oh, this is rich!" He puts his hands over his eyes like he's got a migraine and moans, "Too . . . many . . . jokes . . ."

Soon everyone's laughing. It is kind of funny, really. I mean who wears turtlenecks anyway, except for hockey or skiing? And now they make *dickies*? Why? Who the heck buys a fake turtleneck? That's like mock spam.

Even after everyone else stops, Shane's still laughing so hard he's split the scab on his lip. Tears are running down his cheeks.

Maybe it's the sight of Egghead trying to look all dignified as he stomps away in his torn dickie. Maybe it's just the word *dickie* that did it. Last summer, me and Shane cracked up every time my mom asked if we wanted our wieners boiled or barbequed.

Or maybe Shane just really needs it. A good gut-wrenching-till-your-sides-hurt kind of laugh. 'Cause on some days if you don't laugh like that, you just might cry.

I pat Shane on the back and laugh too, relieved it's over, for now.

Egghead has no idea how much pain that little dickie prevented. And I don't just mean for him.

Dickies. Just another mystery of the universe, I think, watching Egghead and Katie walk down the hall.

That, and girls. Geez, God must have a real sense of humor.

Katie

I got to school early the day of the science fair and went into the gym. I wanted to give myself enough time to set up. The project had kept me pretty busy the last few days, but not busy enough. I couldn't stop thinking about the other day. About *him*. Not Will. Not even Shane.

Devan. I just couldn't get him out of my mind.

Why did he grab me like that? At first, I thought he held me so Shane could take a swing at me. I had never felt so scared. But I don't think that was it. Devan was holding me back. But why? Why wouldn't he let me help Will?

I was terrified then, but now I felt foolish. I hated to admit it, but I used to think Devan liked me. He asked me to be partners. He said I was artistic. And there was something, I can't explain it, just *something* about the way he looked at me.

I set up the boards on an empty table and started ripping strips of duct tape to stick the Styrofoam ant on the top. *Forget about it. Forget about him. Devan Mitchell is a loser, just like Shane. And I don't want to have anything to do with either of them.*

I leafed through the labels I'd written on index cards to find the ones for the ant. Will arrived with the ant farm and set it on the table as Mr. Jackson and the other kids came over to see. The larvae were just starting to get active. Perfect timing.

Dad and I built the new ant farm over the summer. We used an old double-glazed windowpane we found in Granny's shed. We spent a whole night painting tiny road signs on the glass: *Ant X-ing, Yield to Oncoming Ants, Speed Limit 0.005 km/hr, Welcome to Antville.* They got even funnier the more tired we got. Okay, it's not all that funny now, but that night it was hilarious.

Mr. Jackson peered into the glass windows. "Wow, this looks wonderful, guys! Maybe you should stay here with the ant farm during homeroom, Will."

Earlier that week, someone poured Coke in the lab's aquarium and killed all the fish. Another day Mr. Jackson found three pickles in the pig fetuses' jars. Somebody's idea of a joke. Anyhow, I guess Mr. Jackson figured things would be safer if Will stayed behind.

Little did we know how wrong he was.

Devan

I can't believe Shane ditched me. I told him to meet me at my house and help me carry the stuff. It's bad enough I had to make it all myself. But no. He forgets. And to top it off, now I'm late.

Spence is standing by the sign-in sheet waiting to do the morning announcements. *Great.*

"Well now, Mr. Mitchell," he looks at his watch. "All the other participants showed up *on time* and have finished setting up. Deadlines exist for a reason. It wouldn't be fair to the people that—"

Blah blah blah.

For a moment, I think he isn't going to unlock the gym for me, that I had done all that work, all my work *and* Shane's work, for nothing. I must look like I was going to cry or something. Not that I was, of course. But next thing I know, Spence is leading me to the gym.

"Be sure this doesn't happen again," he says, unlocking the side door.

Well, duh! There's only one science fair.

"I've to go do the announcements," he continued. "Lock up behind you, Devan."

I nod and then wander up and down the aisles until I find an empty table over in the corner. Luckily, I'd put most of the boards together at home, so it didn't take long to set the project up.

Spence's voice blasts over the intercom. "Good morning. Here are today's announcements."

I'm taping the last poster board on the wall by the time he tells us to stand for the national anthem. Then I hear it.

"OooOOOOh Caaaa-nada."

I look between the projects behind me to see what moron is singing alone in the gym.

Egghead. I should've known it was him.

He's belting it out like he's at center ice at a hockey game or something, hitting notes beyond human hearing range. Man, dogs must be barking somewhere.

A door slams. The door I was supposed to lock behind me.

"Shut your mouth!" Shane yells, as he and Brad barge in. He grabs the roll of duct tape off the table and sticks a strip across Egghead's mouth.

The singing stops.

"What do we got here?" Brad says, looking at the ant farm. He taps the glass.

Egghead squirms and whimpers the more Brad taps. Brad smiles. He starts pushing the ant farm until it wobbles at the edge of the table. Egghead's eyes are bugging out. If he opened them any bigger, I swear they would've rolled out right there.

"You got something to say?" Shane asks, picking some cards off the table.

Egghead totally ignores Shane and lunges for Brad, hitting him square in the back and sending him flying. Brad's face squeaks across the floor like a wet gym shoe. He rolls onto his elbow and looks up in shock at Egghead standing over him.

Guess he never thought Egghead had it in him. I know I didn't. But Shane only smiles.

"Who do you think you are?" Shane yells, shoving Egghead back into the table. The farm rocks. Egghead can't take his eyes off it, like he's more worried about something happening to it than to him.

"Yeah," Brad echoes, suddenly braver. "Who do *you* think you are?" He scrambles to his feet and twists Egghead's arms behind his back. Shane rips out a strip of duct tape and winds it around Egghead's wrists. They push him between them like a pinball. All Egghead can do is wriggle and grunt.

"I'll tell you who you are, you little maggot." Shane grabs some cards off the table and hooks Egghead's head in his arm like he's going to give him a noogie. He winds the tape around the guy's head. Egghead's pulling away, till Shane punches him in the face and gut.

Finally, Shane steps back to admire his work. Egghead slumps to his knees, snorting hard, trying to get his wind back. He has blood on his shirt from a cut on his cheek. Duct tape is wound around his head like a sweatband and sticking out the top, just over his brow, are two cards.

Egg. Head.

"Ha! Ha!" goes Brad. "Egg. Head. It's Egghead, get it?"

Geez, do I sound that lame?

I'd been looking for Shane all morning. Now I just want him to leave. *Go, just go.* He stopped and turns in my direction. I crouch down. I don't want to be seen, not now.

Shane walks over and flicks his finger at the ant farm. It teeters then tips over the edge. Egghead's eyes go wide.

"NoooOOOOooo!" I shout. But I doubt anybody hears it over the sound of the farm hitting the floor. It smashes in an explosion of glass and splintering wood, shattering right beside Egghead.

Shane and Brad stomp around, squashing any ants lucky enough to survive the crash. They're keeping a tally. Seeing who could kill the most. Egghead's freakin' out, writhing on the floor, totally helpless.

"Let's go," Shane finally says. The bell is about to ring. He heads through the side door I'd forgotten to lock behind me, but Brad stops. He turns and looks back. Right at me.

He knew. The whole time, he knew I was there. Our eyes meet and I know what he's thinking.

Why are you hiding, Dev? You coulda helped us. Why didn't you do something?

Then he runs out after Shane.

I look down at the ant massacre. All that work and time. Gone. Ruined. Just like that. I feel sick to my stomach. Poor Egghead. Poor *Katie.* I totally forgot it was her project too. She is going to be crushed.

Maybe something can be saved, I think. I hope. But I know it's too late. I scan the dirt, smeared ants, and broken glass, and stop short at Egghead's face. He's just lying there. Crying. Looking at me with those eyes. Asking me the very same thing as Brad.

Why are you hiding, Devan? You could have helped me. Why didn't you do something?

Only I didn't have an answer. For either of them.

william james reid

No Difference

I am
not all that different
from you.

Unless you consider that
I am
the only one
who isn't
trying to be the
same.

Katie

When the announcements were over, Mme. Latour asked me to run the attendance sheets down to the office. On the way back, I stopped by the gym to see how Will was doing with the labels. I wanted everything to be perfect. But I knew Will was right. With a project like ours, first place was in the bag.

The gym door was still locked. I yanked on the handles, and then I heard a door slam and someone ran up the stairwell.

The hairs on my neck prickled. Something wasn't right.

I ran to the far door, flung it open, and rushed in. As I rounded the corner to our aisle, something gritty crunched beneath my shoes. And then I saw.

It took a few seconds to take it in. Sand. Shards. Splinters. It was unreal, like watching surgery on TV. My mind just couldn't believe what I was actually seeing.

Until I saw the ants.

They scurried in all directions on the gym floor, frantically searching among the wreckage for a bearing, for each other. I had to do something. I knelt, scooping what I could with my bare hands. Maybe I could save some. Maybe.

A piece of glass jabbed into my palm. But I didn't stop. *If I could just get a container, if I had a food source to attract them, if I . . .*

The few ants I had corralled spilled over my hands in a frenzy. I stopped to pull the shard from my palm. Blood dripped in the dirt. The glass had some writing on it, part of our *Welcome to Antville* sign. My palm throbbed, but I felt numb as the reality hit me.

Antville was gone. The pupae, the larvae, the workers, the queen. All of them.

Gone. Just like that.

Where is Will? I thought, looking around.

I found him beneath the table, lying among dirt, splinters, and dead ants. A few ants crawled over his face. A strip of tape covered his mouth. Another bound his head and held two of my cards. *Egg* and *Head.*

"Oh, Will," I said in a quiet voice. His eyes closed, but it didn't stop the tears. Not his. And not mine.

All was lost.

I helped him up and took off the tape. No matter how gently I tried, it ripped out patches of his hair and made his lips bleed. "Who did this?!" I asked.

Will looked away. I knew he wouldn't name names, and to be honest it could have been anyone. It was only October and already every Grade 9 kid knew Will Reid. Just yesterday he took a fit in the hall, reminded Mr. Jackson about the pop quiz, and knocked the spit bucket all over the brass section in music class. All before third period. So really it *could* have been anyone. But I had my suspicions.

"I'm sorry, Katie. I . . . " His face turned red as he looked away. I knew he felt responsible. In a way, I guess he was. He should have put a stop to all this long ago. "If it wasn't for me this wouldn't have happened," he mumbled.

"You *have* to *do* something about this, Will!" Anger at the whole stupid thing was boiling inside me like a volcano. I was going to blow. "You can't let them do this to you. You have to tell Mr. Spence. If you won't, I will!"

He grabbed my arms. "Don't! Don't tell," he said. "You saw how Shane was when he thought I'd told before. Just imagine what he'd do to me if I really did tell."

I didn't know what to think. Telling might make things worse for Will, but staying silent didn't seem to be helping any either.

"What happened?" Mr. Jackson cried, coming into the gym. "Who did this?"

"I . . . uh . . . I knocked the table." Will lied. "It was an accident."

Mr. Jackson frowned. I could tell he didn't believe Will. Given all the recent pranks in the lab, it wasn't surprising. "Katie?" His eyes searched my face, and as though reading my thoughts he added, "*Ratting* is telling to get someone in trouble. *Reporting* is telling to keep someone safe." He looked at Will and then back at me. "For your own safety, if you know something, you should report it."

I felt torn. Should I say something? "It . . . it was—" Will squeezed my hand and I paused, looking away from Mr. Jackson's eyes. "It was an accident."

"Well, I'm here if you ever change your mind." Mr. Jackson didn't press any further. He had a science fair to run. He looked at his watch. "Let's get this mess cleaned up. The doors open in five minutes."

Will and I swept up the glass, dirt, and dead ants, as if losing them wasn't bad enough. To top it off, we had to sit at the table through the entire fair. Will put on a brave face, despite his blotchy forehead and scabbing lips. He showed the judges the Styrofoam model, but without the ants, our ants; the whole thing was just ridiculous. It took me everything I had not to burst out crying.

I didn't wait around for the results. I rushed home to do the thing I needed most, and wanted least.

To tell Dad all about it.

Devan

"What's your problem?" Shane asks from the back seat of the bus. He's sprawled across it, leaving Brad and me standing.

I shrug. I can't explain it. It's like I'm a kaleidoscope turned an inch too far and suddenly the whole picture is changed. But I don't tell him that. He'd have a field day with that one.

"Is it the *science fair*?" Brad says, with that stupid smirk.

"Don't tell me you're still sore about having to set up on your own." Shane swings his third place medal in a circle so the ribbon wraps around his fingers. Then he swings it the other way.

Brad opens his mouth like he's about to set the record straight. I give him a look. Whatever it said, it shut him up fast.

"We *won!*" Shane brags, like he had anything to do with it. "Man, my mom's gonna freak when she sees this."

The phone is ringing as I unlock the front door. It's Mom. Ever since she started working, she calls every day at 3:45 to ask me the silly questions she asked when she was home all the time.

So how was your day?

Fine.

How was school?

Fine.

What did you do?

Nothing.

I know she'll ask about the science fair today. I don't feel much like talking about it. But I know better than to let the machine pick up. Last time I didn't answer, she called 9-1-1. Two minutes later I got four firemen, two paramedics, and a canine unit at my door, all because I had to take a dump.

I pick it up. "Hello?"

"Hi sweetie, how was your day?"

"Fine."

"What did you do? "

"Nothing."

"How did the science fair go?"

"Good."

"That's nice, dear. Is Em home?" she asks, just as Em's bus pulls away. I don't know how Mom does that. It's like ESP or something. Em opens the front door and sticks her tongue out at me right on cue. Then she runs downstairs to see her rabbit, Lulu.

"Yeah, The Pain is here," I say.

"There are some—"

"Sandwiches in the fridge."

"And can you put the lasagna in at three—"

"Three-fifty for thirty minutes at 5:30. Yeah, Mom. See you later."

"Love you."

"Me too."

I open the fridge and grab two pops and the plate of sandwiches. Mom shrink-wraps everything. The whole second shelf is always full of half empty dishes mummified in plastic wrap. Like we'll ever eat any of it. *Well, you might get hungry when I'm not there,* she says. As if Em will starve to death just 'cause her mother works at Home Depot three nights a week. Em's the fattest kid in Grade 3.

"Em, your sandwich," I call. That kid would spend forever down there with that dumb rabbit.

I sit at the table and bite into my sandwich, but I can't eat. I feel like I've already swallowed a ball of dough. It's just rolling around in my gut. I dunno why the ant farm bothers me so much. After Katie shot me down, I wanted them to lose, more than anything. But not this way.

What would have happened if I had been with Shane this morning? I don't have to think about that too long to know I would have been holding Egghead's wrists, or wrapping the tape, or taking a shot. It makes me sick to think it.

Katie looked so sad during the fair. I'd never seen her like that. Egghead managed, but I knew the truth. I'd seen it in his eyes when he was lying on the ground.

He hurt. A lot. And it wasn't just from getting his butt kicked.

I take the medal out of my pocket and look at my bronze reflection. I'd won lots of medals for sports but never for science. I should be proud. But I'm not. I know we don't deserve third. Egghead and Katie's project should have won first. It was the best one, before it got trashed. That would have bumped us down to fourth. And fourth placers don't get medals.

"What's that?" Em asks, sliding into her chair. Salt lines mark her cheeks where tears dried. Looks like she didn't have such a great day either.

"Just an award," I say, getting up to toss it, and my sandwich, in the trash. But I stop. "Here, Em." I slip the red and white ribbon over her head. "For being the best rabbit owner. Congratulations."

Em smiles so big, she looks like she might burst. She can't take her eyes off the medal. She can hardly chew with that big, goofy grin on her face. Even I feel a bit better.

Funny how something little can make such a big difference.

william james reid

Salty Peas

"Pass the peas, Will."
He can reach the china bowl, but I pass it.

Tick-tock
Tick-tock
The clock seems so much louder
Since Mom died.

Mom knew I hated peas.
I'd get two scoops of potatoes,
Slathered in hot gravy,
Just the way I like it.

Tick-tock.

"How was your day?" he says, not wanting to know.
His face is closed.
Cold.
Wooden.
Like her casket.

Tick-tock.

"Fine."

I open my mouth hungry for answers.
Should I hurt this much?
Did you love her too?
Do you love me?

He raises his eyebrow.
And all I can say is:

"Pass the salt."

I eat my cold, salty, peas in silence.

Just the way he likes it.

Katie

After the day I'd had, I thought things couldn't get worse. When I opened the front door and saw Granny's expression, I knew they could.

Much worse.

"Your father's in the hospital," she said, grabbing her coat. "C'mon now, I'll take you to see him."

Granny was always matter-of-fact about things. If you got a bad haircut, she'd tell you. If she didn't like your friends, she'd tell you. She even told me when my armpits got sort of smelly this summer. She took me to Quinn's and bought me deodorant that smelled like baby powder. Although, after twelve years of proving I'm not a baby, the last thing I wanted was to smell like one.

That was just Granny. She always spoke to me like an adult and never said "I'll tell you when you're older." But, as we walked to her car, something in her face made me think I didn't want to hear what she didn't want to say.

My stomach sank as we came to the hospital doors labeled ICU. If Dad was in the Intensive Care Unit, I knew things weren't good. Granny squeezed my hand as we walked past Room 107 where Grampa had stayed. It must have been hard to see her only son grow sicker with the same thing six years after her husband had died. I squeezed her hand back. We understood. Neither of us wanted to be here, but both of us were glad the other was.

Dad had been in and out of hospital most of the summer. During his last stay, the head nurse, Maureen, made me an honorary nurse. I learned how to take Dad's vitals: nurse talk for heart rate, temperature, and blood pressure.

My shoes squeaked on the shiny floor as we traveled the long hall, passing one room after another. Each one held its own story, but the only one I was concerned about was in Room 112. I pushed the door open expecting to hear Dad's old, "Hey kiddo!" But he just lay there, hooked up to all kinds of machines, eyes closed.

"Dad?" My voice sounded loud and strange, like it wasn't even coming from my body. He slowly opened his eyes and looked at me. He said something, muffled under the plastic mask on his face.

Granny told him not to worry about me. That she had moved her stuff to the house and I'd be fine. My head was spinning.

Why did she say that? Was he going to be in here long this time?

Maureen came in on her silent shoes, checked a beeping machine and left. She didn't even say hi.

Dad has been like this before. It's just another bad spell. Why is everyone acting so weird?

Granny pulled up a chair beside Dad's bed and put her hand over his. Grampa's black rosary beads wove in and out of her old fingers like knitting wool.

A sure sign that life was unraveling.

With each bad spell, Dad's recoveries were worse. Slower. Longer. He hardly got the chance to get back to his old self before the next one hit. But he never gave up. He reminded me of a little kid trying to run up a slide, climbing and slipping and climbing and slipping. Never noticing how close they really were to the end.

"Oh, honey . . . the science fair. How was it?" Dad said weakly, starting to wake up a bit more. I wished I had a first place medal to show him. I even considered lying. After all, we should have won.

"What happened?" he asked. He could tell something wasn't right. I couldn't lie to him. I just couldn't. So I told him. All of it. About the science fair, about Will and how people always picked on him, and how I always had to stand up for him or no one would, not even himself. I told him about Jenna, Shane, and I even told him all about Devan.

"Why does it all have to change?" My voice cracked, but I did everything I could not to cry. "Why can't it just stay the way it was last year?"

Dad smiled. "Katie, nothing ever stays the same. That's life, honey."

"But I want it to," I said. I knew I sounded like a sulky little kid, but I really felt scared. My friends. My old teachers. My old school. My old life. I loved those things. I didn't want to let go.

Maureen came in with her arms full of supplies. She unhooked the plastic bag hanging up behind Dad's bed and replaced it with a new one.

"See?" Dad joked. "Even I need a change."

Maureen smiled. "I think your dad needs to rest now." Nurse talk for: *he is not doing too good.* "Why don't you come back in about an hour or so?"

Granny patted Dad's hand. "We'll be back in a bit, John. Try and get some sleep." Dad squeezed her hand and nodded.

"Don't worry, Katie-girl," he said, stroking my hair as I kissed his cheek. "It'll all be just fine. I promise."

How can he promise that? I thought, following Granny down the hall to the elevators. *I wanted to win and make Dad proud. I wanted to protect Will from Shane. I wanted to save the ants. And I couldn't.*

We stepped into the elevator. Granny put her arm around my shoulder and my tears came as the door closed.

Wanting something doesn't make it true. I know. Because more than anything, I wanted my dad to be okay.

Devan

Stopping at the table where Egghead is eating lunch alone as usual, Shane picks up a hard-boiled egg.

"Let me help you with that." He shoves the egg, shell and all, into Egghead's mouth and jams his jaw shut with the heel of his palm. White guck oozes out of Egghead's mouth like a big zit. He's gagging and coughing egg shrapnel all over the table.

"Hey, scrambled Egghead," Shane says.

Brad laughs like it's the funniest thing he's ever heard. "Get it?" He elbows me. "*Scrambled* Egghead!"

Yeah. I get it. But it's not funny anymore.

"You know what goes well with egg, Dev?" Shane asks, taking a pudding cup out of Egghead's lunch bag. We all know who'll end up wearing it.

Egghead looks at me. The same way he looked at me in the gym.

Why is he looking at me like that? I'm not doing it. It's Shane. Shane's the one.

But I can't get rid of the sick feeling in my stomach.

I've got to get out of here.

I cross the caf and shove the side door leading outside to the back steps. *Bam!* I slam into Katie, again, landing her on her butt.

"Boy, you really have it in for me, don't you?" she snaps. She doesn't let me help her up. Instead she just turns and stays sitting on the top step.

"Man, Katie, I'm so sorry." I feel like total crap. She gives me this dirty look, but then she gets this smile and looks away.

"You have egg on your face."

"Oh," I sit beside her and wipe my face. "Shane's feeding Egghead."

"I know."

"I'm surprised you're not in there helping Egghead," I say.

She shrugs. "I'm surprised you're not in there helping Shane."

We just sit for a few seconds.

"I *had* to get out of there!" we both say at the same time, and then grin. It feels good.

Big snowflakes float down and cover the empty football field. Everything is so quiet. Like there is no one else in the world at that moment but the two of us.

"He's not your problem." I say. "Will, I mean."

She tilts her head and smiles at me. I guess I never called him by his real name before.

"I know," she leans back on her hands and stares out at the field. "Nobody understands him. He's just—different. Nobody knows what it's like to be him."

"Who knows what anyone's life is like, really," I say, thinking of Shane. No one knows what he's dealing with at home. Not that it's an excuse or anything. But no one really knows. "We all have our problems, right?"

She looks away and chews on her bottom lip.

Did I say something wrong?

The wind blows up the steps and she shivers.

"Here," I take off my sweatshirt and throw it around her shoulders. She wraps it around her. I wish my arms were still in it.

"Nice project, by the way," she says, looking over at me. "I learned a lot about animation."

"Thanks."

"Third place, too." She looks impressed.

"I'm not really a winner." I mutter.

"Sure you are," she says, like I'm acting all humble.

If only she knew. I'm *not* a winner. I'm the loser who stood by and did nothing.

Katie

"So I should wear the red dress, right?" Jenna asked, for the hundredth time. She had let me tag along with her and Isabella to help her pick the perfect outfit.

"Yes. Red." I said. Like it mattered either way. Tonight was the Christmas dance. And somehow she had gotten it into her head that she would be dancing with Mike Montana.

"But Mike's favorite color is blue," Isabella said from under an armload of dresses in the corner of the tiny change room.

Jenna whined. I groaned. I should have just stayed home. Go, Granny had said, practically shoving me out the door, *girl fun is just what you need.* Since when was an hour-long debate about Mike Montana's favorite colors fun?

"Look, Jenna," I said, losing patience. "Mike also likes the Ottawa Senators but you're not going to wear goalie pads and a helmet to the dance, now are you?"

Jenna looked at Isabella. Like it might actually be a possibility.

"That's it." I grabbed my coat. "I'm out of here."

"What's her problem?" Isabella asked in a voice loud enough for me to hear. "No date for the dance? There's always *Egghead*."

I never liked that girl. Granny wouldn't either.

They giggled as I left. Whispering to each other about how I wasn't helping my case with *those* clothes and *that* hairstyle.

Yeah. Whatever.

"That you?" Granny asked, surprised I was back so soon. She came down the front hall and caught me just standing, staring at my reflection in the mirror.

I had to be honest. The girls were right about one thing. I did look kind of grungy. From my frizzy hair to my salt-stained jean hems, I wasn't much to look at.

"Granny," I asked, bracing myself for the truth. "Am I . . . pretty?"

"'Course you are, girl." She tilted her head. "Mind you, you could do with a bit of fixing up. Maybe a trim." She looked at her reflection beside mine. "I'm looking a bit haggard myself. What say we head out for some real girl fun, just you and me?"

We spent the rest of the afternoon back at the mall—only this time I had a blast.

"Give us something new and exciting," Granny told Rhonda, the hairstylist. "Just not too exciting."

Rhonda cut and colored Granny's salt-and-pepper bun into a cute little bob just below the chin. Granny looked like a new woman.

I didn't get mine dyed. Rhonda said I didn't need to, that I had natural highlights. That people actually paid to get their hair my reddish color. We talked about school and shopping as she cut long strands of hair. I was a bit anxious when I saw all the hair on the floor, but by the time she finished drying it, I looked like a movie star. I never knew my hair could do that.

"Now you're all set for the dance tonight," Rhonda said putting down the brush.

"What?" Granny said. "A dance? You didn't tell me about that."

I hadn't planned on going.

"Yeah," Rhonda continued. "The Christmas formal. You should see the nice tie I got my Shane. He's about your age, honey. You know him?"

I gawked at her in the mirror. *Shane's mom?* She didn't look a thing like him, maybe because she was nice and smiled a lot.

"Well, you tell him I said to go on up and ask that Erin girl to dance," Rhonda winked. "Had a crush on her since September, only he's too shy to admit it."

I nearly choked. *Shane likes Erin?*

Granny paid Rhonda, gave her a nice big tip. Which was good. Anyone who has to live with Shane must need all the perks they can get.

Granny insisted on "suiting me up" for the dance. She even bought me a new lip gloss and mascara. I kept telling her I wasn't going, but she wouldn't hear of it.

I tried on the green dress. It wasn't like the things Jenna and Isabella chose. Mine was dark green velvet to just above the knee, with a scoop neck. Plain and simple.

Granny clasped her hands together and brought them to her chin as I came out. Her eyes filled up. She looked at me for a moment, then took off her pearls and put them around my neck. The little balls felt warm and heavy against my skin.

"There now," she said, turning me towards the mirror.

I couldn't believe it. The dress. The hair. The pearls. The young woman in the mirror looked like someone from an old photo. Someone I always loved and never knew.

"So Katie," Granny whispered in my ear. "Does that answer your question?"

I looked at my reflection.

"Yes." My eyes filled with tears. "I *am* pretty. I look just like Mom."

Devan

"Where'd you take off to at lunch today?" Shane asks after school. We're playing street hockey outside my house. He winds up for the shot.

"I dunno," I say.

He stops and rests both hands on the end of his stick and smirks at me. I dunno how he does it, but he can always tell I'm lying.

"You went to see a *girl*, didn't you?"

My cheeks burn. "No."

"You did! I can tell," he runs around the back of the net where I can't see him. Then dekes in the back corner. "*Score!!* That's eight *nothing*, my man!"

"Well, it's kinda hard for me to score when I'm always in nets, *my man*," I say flicking the ball out.

"Who is she?" He asks, shooting high and left.

I stop it dead in my glove. "You don't know her." This

time it's really the truth. He doesn't know her.

"Is she hot?"

"I guess. She's nice."

"Nice?" he says, like it's a bad thing. He scores on a slapshot then wipes his runny nose on the back of his mitt. "Well, whatever. So listen," he chucks the stick on the top of the net and starts walking home. "I'll see you at 7:30."

"For what?" I ask.

"For what? Listen to you, Romeo, like you didn't know. The dance, loser. Tonight's the Christmas Dance. Didn't you ask your *girlfriend*?"

I shake my head.

"Great!" he yells from halfway down the block. "We'll pick you up at seven!"

And before I can say anything, he's gone.

"You should have told me about it earlier, Devan." Mom complains as she rummages through my closet. I'm sorry now that I mentioned the dance. She's making a big deal of it.

"This is fine. I'll just wear this." I say, stretching my arms out. I wore this shirt to Aunt Maureen's wedding this summer. But I don't remember it being this tight.

"It's too small for you," Em says, sitting on the edge of my bed. "It looks silly."

"Who asked you? Get out of my room."

"If you'd told me about this earlier, I could've picked you up something." Mom pulls out another shirt. It's even smaller than this one.

"I wasn't *planning* on going," I answer, for the tenth time. This collar is choking me.

Dad walks in and leans on the door frame. "Going where?"

"Do you even *know* how to dance?" Em asks me.

"I thought I told you to get out of my room."

"A dance?" Dad says. He starts shaking his hips and snapping his fingers. Mom tries to sidestep past him, only he keeps blocking her, pretending she's dancing with him and not really trying to escape. Laughing, Mom shoves his chest, pushing him out into the hall where he keeps dancing. "Oh, yeah," he goes, "I still got it."

He looks pathetic and he *knows* how to dance. There's no way I'm going to embarrass myself like that. Besides, I don't even have something to wear.

"Forget it." I pull the shirt off. "Just forget it. I'm not going."

"Don't you want to dance with your *gir-r-r-rlfriend*?" Em teases.

My face burns. "Shut up, Pain." I throw the shirt at her.

Dad finally tells her to hit the bricks and winks at me.

"What?" I say.

"Nothing." He smirks.

I hear him and The Pain sing their way down the stairs. "Devan has a girlfriend . . . Devan has a girlfriend . . ."

Ten minutes later Mom's taking pictures of me and Shane standing by the Christmas tree. I'm wearing Dad's blue shirt. I had to roll up the sleeves to make it fit. I drew the line at the tie. I knew Shane wouldn't be wearing one either.

"Look at you, just look at you," Mom says, all choked up. "What handsome young men . . ."

"Are we done now?" I ask. She takes three more.

"Okay, Anne," Dad finally says, "I think we've got enough for a whole scrapbook there."

Shane and I make a break for it—if I don't get out of there soon, Mom will start washing my face with spit.

Katie

Jenna's mom drove. The whole way there all Jenna talked about was Mike. Isabella didn't seem to mind. If talking about her brother kept someone hanging on her every word, she was more than happy to spill. Of course, Jenna lapped it up like someone dying of thirst. And neither of them seemed to care that their entire friendship was a fake.

The gym swallowed us in soft lights and loud music. Guys stood in circles, yanking on their stiff collars and tight ties. Girls wobbled by on their new high heels, like little kids on ice skates. I danced with Jenna and Isabella, glad I listened to Granny about getting the comfy shoes.

Then I saw him through the crowd. Devan.

I couldn't believe he came. Not that he wasn't allowed to. I mean, it was his school too. He stood on the other side of the gym with his hands in his pockets. He looked so different all dressed up. Taller. Older. His blue shirt, unbuttoned at the collar, was rolled at the sleeves. He looked so comfortable. So good. Shane said something to him and he laughed. What a great smile.

He was still smiling when he turned and looked at me. It was like we were the only two in the gym. My heart pounded, my stomach fizzed. No matter what my brain said, my body wasn't listening. I couldn't even look away. Then, the crowd moved and blocked our view.

A slow song started to play and he broke through the crowd, heading my way.

Is he coming to ask me?

"He will! He will!" Isabella squealed. I turned to see her run back to Jenna and me. I hadn't even noticed that she'd left. "Mike says he'll dance with my friend! Okay, okay! Here he comes."

Jenna's face went white. She looked like she was going to collapse. I felt kind of the same, knowing Devan was headed this way.

"Hey," a deep voice said from behind us, "wanna dance?"

Isabella's mouth dropped. Jenna turned and let out a tiny squeak. When I looked around I realized why.

It was Mike Montana. Only he wasn't looking at her.

He was looking at me.

"Hello, Katie," Will said, totally unaware of what he'd just walked in on.

"I . . . uh . . . I promised this one to someone else," I blurted to Mike. Jenna glared at me as I grabbed Will by the elbow and practically dragged him onto the dance floor.

Devan walked right past us. He didn't even look at me. *God, I am such an idiot. He didn't want to dance with me.* I watched him open the door. *He just wanted to go to the washroom.*

Devan

I take a detour to the can so it won't look like what it is. That I'm some loser who just walked across the whole dance floor for nothing.

I'm still kicking myself for not telling her what really happened the day of the science fair. Will might have told her Shane trashed her project and kicked his butt, but Katie doesn't know that I stood by and let it all happen. Somehow, being a chicken doesn't sound any better than being a bully.

I can't believe I was going to ask her to dance. It's just . . . she looked so nice, and I thought she was smiling at me. Next thing I know I'm like halfway across the floor.

Just as well, I guess. Shane would've never let me live that down.

I check myself in the washroom mirror. Like I even had a chance. After a few minutes, I go back to the gym, ready for a razzing from Shane. Only he's not there. He's on the floor dancing with Erin. Even Brad's dancing with someone. Shoving my hands in my pockets, I lean against the wall and watch Katie dance.

She looks so great. I'm not surprised some Grade 10 guy was asking her too. But she turned even him down for Will.

Man, she must really like the guy.

william james reid

Katie

She isn't like other girls.
She doesn't
gossip,
or giggle.

She smiles a lot.
She even smiles at me.

She listens.
She hears.
She knows.
She says what no one else will:

"I'll be your science fair partner."

"Get a grip, Will."

"Leave him alone, Shane."

I don't know if she's pretty.
But she sure is
beautiful.

Mostly because she is
nothing

like other girls.

Katie

Will danced like Frankenstein. He kept stepping on my toes and counting, "One-two-three, one-two-three," under his breath. People pointed. Some laughed. Maybe it was just my imagination but the whispers sounded like *Missus-Egghead-Missus-Egghead-Missus-Egghead.*

The music finally stopped. I figured the night's humiliation was over, until a spotlight shone on Will and me. My stomach sank and I realized it was all just beginning.

"And here are tonight's winners of our spotlight dance." The DJ was standing beside us shouting into his mike. He handed Will an envelope. "Congratulations, you two. It's a romantic dinner for two at Mexicasa."

Everyone started whooping and hollering, like this was good news.

"So, who is the happy couple?" the DJ asked, putting the microphone in front of us. I just wanted to shrivel up and disappear. But not Will.

"I'm William James Reid!" he yelled. The mike squealed. The crowd started chanting.

"*Egg*-head! *Egg*-head! *EGG*-HEAD!!"

Will raised his clasped hands above his head like a total idiot and the place went wild. Couldn't he see? Didn't he know they were all only making fun of him. Of me? Everyone laughed and cheered as Will bowed to all four corners.

"And who," asked the DJ, "is your *lovely* girlfriend?"

"OooooOOOoooO!" went the crowd.

I wanted to die.

"Well she—" Will began.

"I'm *not* his *girlfriend!*" I shrieked. "I don't even *like* him."

I wanted it back right after I said it. But with the mike up in my face, the truth bounced loud and hard around the gym walls before totally crushing Will.

He slumped as it sunk in, but he never took his eyes off me. I saw them go from shock, to disbelief, and finally pain. God, I felt like I'd just kicked a puppy.

"Will, I—" I started to say, searching for a way to say what I really meant. That I didn't like him *that* way. As if that would make it any better.

But before I could say anything more, he turned and ran out.

Everyone burst out laughing. Everyone but me.

I was never a great friend to Will, I admit it. But nothing, nothing was worse than what I had just done. I stepped out of the spotlight and pushed through the crowd—horrified at the realization.

I was one of them now.

william james ʀeid

Katie Part II

I have seen
a queen
eat
some of her
smallest eggs

just
to stay
alive.

Survival
is a
natural instinct.

Only
I did not realize
I was such a

small
egg.

Devan

"Holy crap, I still can't believe that." Shane shakes his head. "Man, she burned him big time."

I can't believe it myself, really. I kind of felt for Egghead. Imagine getting dissed like that in front of the whole gym. It could've been me up there with her in that spotlight.

Shane's mom is late picking us up. Everyone else is long gone.

"Come on," he says, flipping up his collar against the cold. "Let's take the bus."

She pulls up ten minutes later. "Sorry, boys," she says, as we get in.

My butt is so frozen in these damn pants I can't even tell if I'm sitting on the seat.

"What took you so long to—" Shane asks. Then stops.

She's looking at us sideways, hoping we won't see the shiner she's got under all that makeup. I turn and look out the window.

"So," she continues real perky, "how was the dance?"

"Fine." Shane glares at her.

"Did you ask Erin?" She takes out a cigarette and pushes in the lighter. Her hands are shaking. Something tells me it's not from the cold.

"Mom—"

"I'll bet she thought you looked real sharp." She shoves the lighter again, but it keeps popping out. She jams it in with the heel of her hand.

"Mom!"

"This thing's trash—"

"It's not trash," Shane explodes. "Riley is trash! Only *trash* would hurt a girl."

"He just has a problem with his temper is all," she says. "Inside, he's a good man. Riley loves me, Shane."

"Yeah? Well he has a funny way of showing it." Shane snaps. He looks her over. "Maybe you're the trash for letting him treat you like that!"

His mom's cigarette drops. She grips the wheel with both hands and we drive in silence for a while. I can't believe Shane talked to her like that, or that she let him.

No one speaks the rest of the way.

The car finally pulls up to my place. I thank Ms. Duran for the ride. She smiles, but her eyes are full of tears. She seems more hurt by Shane's words than Riley's fist.

"See ya, Shane," I get out of the car. Shane just grunts. I watch them drive into the cold night.

I don't get why he treats his mom like that. Shane loves his mom. A lot. Only he sure has a funny way of showing it.

I guess he never learned any different.

Katie

Granny and I tried to make the holidays like old times, even though we spent them at the hospital. We played Christmas music. We even brought in a foot-high tree to decorate. Dad said it looked like a Charlie Brown reject. He was right, it was pitiful. But at least it made him smile.

On New Year's Eve we sat around Dad's room just listening to Christmas music. Granny started a few card games, but I couldn't stop thinking about school. Will had been avoiding me. And I couldn't blame him. I still hadn't apologized. I wasn't sure how. I'd broken something much more valuable than an ant farm. I had broken Will's heart.

How do I apologize for that?

Even Jenna had been giving me the cold shoulder. She was still angry that Mike asked me to dance. Like it was my fault. The fact that I danced with Will instead just made things worse. I couldn't win.

I used to love school. But the way things had been going I couldn't wait for the Christmas break, not for the presents, just for the escape. I wanted to crawl under my quilt and stay there.

Elvis started singing "Blue Christmas." It echoed around the hospital room. Tears swam in my eyes. I'd never noticed it was a sad song before. When "I'll Be Home for Christmas" started, Granny got up and turned off the CD, saying something about saving batteries.

Last Christmas break, we did all our favorite traditions on Brayside farm, like going cross-country skiing all day and staying up all night to watch the New Year's Eve countdown. I always slept in till about noon New Year's Day, waking up to the warm smell of Dad's famous breakfast. He made it every year: bacon, sausage, and a "mega pancake" as big as a puddle and just as runny. I always loved the holidays.

But this year was different. Much different.

"Here's to another year," Granny said, raising her glass.

"Cheers," Dad raised his as high as the IV tubes would allow. He smiled and sipped his juice. "Isn't this nice? Just the three of us, just like old times."

We played cards for a bit, then Scrabble. By the time the ball dropped in New York, Dad and Granny were sound asleep.

I brought in the New Year on my own.

Devan

"Once you have your equipment and lift tickets," Panetta yells to the crowd as we get off the school bus, "you can head on up the hills. Be back at the bus by four o'clock." Everyone cheers. We've been waiting for this day all Winter Carnival. Ski Day.

The line is moving so slow, we still haven't even made it inside the lodge. I told Shane we should've sat at the front of the bus. But he never listens to me. Tons of kids have got their stuff, some even started their lessons, and we're stuck standing last in line like idiots.

Shane shoves his mitts in his pocket and makes a snowball with his bare hands. That melt-in-your-palm, hard, heavy baseball of ice kind. Those babies sting.

"Watch this." He winds up and whips it over at five cross-country geeks lined up for their lesson. It clocks the first kid in the shoulder. He tumbles into the next guy and they drop like dominoes. Brad laughs.

"Come on, Dev," Shane says tossing me his next ice-ball. He points out another group. "I got five with one shot. Beat that."

"Nah," I drop it and squish it under my boot.

"What? Ya chicken?" Brad laughs.

Oh, he's asking for it. With both hands, I shove his chest and send him flying backwards into the snow-bank. The fall knocks the wind out of him, that and the fact that I slam my weight on him. I flip him facedown and ram that smirk of his into the snow.

"Not so funny now, eh, Brad? Not so funny!"

I shove handfuls of snow into his face with a bit more force than I had planned. But it feels good. Brad's face looks like a raw steak by the time I let him go. I brush the snow from my mitts, glad I finally shut him up. He's all talk, that guy.

"Atta boy, Dev." Shane smiles. "For a second there I thought you were going soft on us."

I clench my jaw and head over to the rental booth. I don't know what makes me angrier—that I lost control or that Shane enjoyed it. He thinks he knows me so well.

Finally, we reach the front of the line and get our equipment. Shane gets a snowboard. So does Brad, of course. I get skis.

"Make wise choices today, boys," Panetta says, giving us our passes. Whatever the hell that means. Probably read it in *Teaching for Dummies.*

"C'mon, race you to the lift!" Shane takes off with Brad close behind. It's a two-man lift, so the last one there is the odd man out. But I don't mind riding alone for a change.

In fact, I kind of like it.

Katie

I love downhill skiing. Dad taught me when I was little. In his twenties, he'd worked as a ski instructor to pay for university. Granny always said he only did it to impress girls. "Well, it worked, didn't it?" he'd say with a grin. That was how he met my mom. Only legend has it, she saved him.

I tagged along behind Isabella and Jenna all day. The chairlift kept reinforcing that three was a crowd.

"Stand here," the lift attendant said, pushing me back as Jenna and Isabella swung up on their chair. "We have to wait for another single."

I stood for ages watching everyone else go up the mountain. Some had even made it back for a second run. Suddenly, the attendant waved me over.

"Single, single, come on, let's go," he said, like he'd been waiting on me all this time. I sidestepped over beside the other single just as the chair rounded the corner and scooped us up.

"Finally," I sat and pulled the guard bar down.

"Hey, Katie." The guy beside me pulled off his goggles. It was Devan.

"Oh, hi." My stomach twisted, as the chair lifted off the ground. I swallowed hard. "I hardly recognized you, without Shane."

He pointed at the chair in front of us holding Shane and Brad. Shane gave me the finger—at least I think he did. It was in a mitt.

The chairlift shuddered to a stop. Someone had probably sprawled across the ramp trying to get off the lift. We swung in the cold air. The sun sparkled on the snowy tips of the pines below our skis. Neither of us spoke. The lift started up again.

"Sorry about . . . about your ant farm," he finally mumbled into his scarf. "Do you know what happened?"

"No. Will doesn't want to talk about it."

Devan seemed relieved. "Well, you guys would've won first. Your ant farm was awesome. I mean—it probably was."

"Yeah, it's not just losing the fair. That ant farm meant a lot to me. My dad helped me make it." Tears burned in the corner of my eyes. I looked away, embarrassed that I was still feeling upset about it. "I'm surprised I made it through the fair without crying. But Will put on a brave face."

"Not bad, considering his face had tape burn," Devan said and laughed.

Devan

She stiffens beside me. Something's wrong. She won't even look at me now.

What? What did I say?

I replay the conversation. *Tape burn.* That's it! Of course! How could I have been so stupid? Only someone who'd *been there* that morning would know about the tape. As far as Katie is concerned that's her, Egghead, and whoever did it.

She thinks I did it. The tape, the ant farm, all of it. Great, just great. I shiver in the blowing snow. *I'll be lucky if she ever speaks to me again.*

The chair finally reaches the top of the hill. Neither of us says anything.

Some guy in a goofy red hat with a wicked huge pom-pom is blocking the ramp. One ski is on his shoulder and he's bending over to pick up his pole. The lift operator is going crazy, shouting at the guy to get out of the way as the people on the chair in front of us hit the ramp.

"What?" The guy turns, swinging the ski on his shoulder around. It whacks one of the skiers in the back. He reaches out to help her and clotheslines the other one with his pole. Total Three Stooges. Now three bodies block the ramp.

The man working the lift runs back to his hut and slams the brake. I hear him shouting, in French, I think. Only he's conjugating some verbs Madame Latour hadn't taught us. He grabs the guy in the red hat by the jacket, drags him off the ramp, and dumps him in the snow bank. The other two take off down the hill.

Katie and I ski down the ramp and pass the guy. His skis are pointing in opposite directions, but they are on at least. He's bent over, snapping up a boot. Red threads are falling out of his pom-pom.

He barely made it down the ramp. How the hell will he survive the actual hill?

I'm surprised someone that inexperienced would be dumb enough to ski without taking lessons first. He sits up.

It's Egghead.

Somehow, I'm not surprised at all.

Katie

I figured Shane was behind the ant farm disaster, but I had hoped Devan wasn't.

How could I like someone like that? I thought, watching him ski down the ramp. *Someone like Shane.*

Shane and Brad swerved in front of me forcing me to stop.

"Comin', Dev?" Shane asked, looking right at me.

Devan hesitated.

Just then Will flew past us looking like a seizure on skis, poles swinging, skis shuddering as he picked up speed.

"Snowplow!" I shouted over the laughter of the chair-lift spectators. He might have tried to turn his tips together, but he ended up crossing them and flipping face first into the snow.

I skied over to see if he was okay. His face was red raw, bleeding in spots where ice had grazed. The snow plugs rammed up his nostrils were quickly melting. He looked stunned. Thankfully, he hadn't really hurt anything other than his pride.

"Here." I offered a hand, but he shrugged me away. He dug in a pole and tried to stand. "Will, try turning your skis—"

"I know, I know," he said, though I seriously doubted it. He obviously didn't even know enough to *not* get up when his skis faced downhill. Within seconds, they'd shot out from under him and he was flat on his back.

Shane, Brad, and Devan stopped beside us spraying snow in Will's face. Shane picked Will's hat and pulled out a loose thread.

"Give it back," Will said, finally on his feet.

"What—*this*?" Shane shook it. Bits of pom-pom scattered on the snow. He pulled another thread. Stitches around the top began unravelling.

"*Don't!*" Will cried. "My mother made—you're *wrecking* it!" He lunged at Shane, forgetting about the skis on his feet until they tripped him up.

Brad laughed.

"Just give him his hat, Shane," Devan said.

Shane stared at him in shock. Then his eyes narrowed. Devan's jaw clenched; he didn't look away.

"If you want it so badly, Egghead, go get it," Shane said pitching it over the ridge and down Devil's Hill. The weight of the pom-pom carried the hat until it slid to a stop halfway down the moguls. He looked back at Will. "Whaddya say? You chicken?"

"What came first, the chicken or the Egghead?" Brad flapped his arms. "Brawk, Brawk."

Will stood. He looked between Shane, the hat, and the hill, like he was actually considering it. There was no way he could do it, not Will, not in one piece anyway. What was he thinking?

"Devil's Hill is an advanced run," Devan said, nodding at the sign. "It's not for beginners."

Shane glared at Devan. "That's right," Shane said, turning back to Will. "*We* could all do it. But not a chicken spit like you."

"Bwawk, Bwawk," Brad clucked.

"Heck, I'll even give you ten bucks if you do it," Shane said, as if ten dollars meant anything to Will. "Who knows," Shane added to clinch the deal, "you might even win back your *girlfriend* too."

Everyone stared at me, even Will. My mouth opened to say, "I'm not his girlfriend," but I caught myself this time and closed it.

I wanted to scream. To shout out how stupid everyone was acting, especially Will. That he didn't have to prove anything to anyone, that everyone knows a beginner shouldn't ski Devil's Hill, that he was acting like an idiot! I should have told him I'd get his damn hat, but I didn't. I kept quiet.

I looked at Will standing on the edge, and I never said a thing to stop him.

william james Reid

The Peak

At the peak
of panic,
every animal
must choose between

fight or flight.

I am afraid
of doing something.

I am more afraid
of doing nothing.

At the edge
of action,
every animal
feels that fear.

It's what we do with it
that counts.
And I am tired
of
being afraid.

Devan

"Holy crap! He's going for it!" Brad says.

Egghead takes off. He hits the first mogul hard, and doesn't have a chance to get his balance before slamming into the next. He's swinging his arms and poles in crazy circles, doing everything he can just to stay on his feet.

It would have been better if he hadn't.

We all see it coming. Even Shane stops laughing as Will ricochets off that last mogul and straight into the—

"TREE!"

I don't know who shouts it. But I'll never forget the sickening *cr-r-r-a-ack!* as Egghead hits. It sounds wrong. Way wrong.

His ski jams into a low branch, bowing his leg as his body twists. Something snaps. He drops flat on his back and slides over a few moguls. Up and down. Up and down, like he's floating on a white lake.

He's okay, I tell myself. *Just resting. Just fooling.*

"NO!! Someone get the ski patrol!" Katie screams, and races down the hill.

Shane takes off for the chairlift shack. I follow Katie, thankful that she knows the run. The hill is even steeper than it looks. All that matters is getting to Egghead, even though a part of me is afraid of what we'll find.

"Don't move him." Katie kneels beside him taking off her mitts. He's still, too still. She leans over and listens at his mouth, then touches his neck for a pulse.

"Is he—?" I can't even say it.

"He's breathing."

I take a breath, surprised I was holding it. Then I take off my skis. The snow crunches loudly under my boots as I step in closer.

Egghead's eyes are closed. A wicked golf ball lump is growing on his forehead. Blood, a lot of blood, is running from his nose and the cuts on his cheek, turning the snow beneath into cherry slush. But it's the blood slowly dripping like red candle wax out of his ear that freaks me out.

He lost one ski; the other is broken. *If it did that to his ski, what the hell did it do to his bones?* His legs bend where there are no joints making his boots stick out at weird angles. My stomach churns and my head spins just thinking about it.

Get a grip, Dev. I look away and breathe deep, hoping the cold air will keep me from throwing up or passing out. Not knowing what else to do, I bend over and pick up his hat.

Oh yeah, you're a great help.

Katie lifts his eyelids with her thumb. One eye looks as if it's having a pupil eclipse.

"Will," she says in a calm voice. "It's Katie. You've had an accident. But the ski patrol are on their way. You're going to be okay, Will." She touches his left cheek, about the only thing that doesn't look hurt. "You're going to be okay."

I hope he hears her. Maybe she's given him some kind of hope, even if we both know it's a lie.

He isn't going to be okay. Ever.

Katie

It felt like forever, but the ski patrol finally came and took over. They bound his legs, strapped him to a backboard and tied him to a sled before slowly maneuvering down the rest of Devil's Hill. Mr. Panetta waited with an ambulance at the bottom.

I just wanted to sit somewhere and cry. My hands were still shaking. *Oh God, Will,* I thought as the paramedics slid him, sled and all, into the back. *Be okay.*

Shane and Brad joined Devan. I took off my skis and walked over, not sure what I wanted to say. But I had to say something.

Devan still held Will's hat in his hands. I snatched it away and glared at Shane.

"You . . . you owe Will ten dollars," I said, my words like ice. "He made it to the bottom. He made it—" my voice cracked. I stared at each of them. "You owe him."

Devan

The look on Katie's face kills me.

I want to tell her she's wrong. That *I* didn't do anything. Shane did it all, the underwear, the ant farm, and now . . . this.

But I don't say anything. She is right. I do owe Will.

Shane did the pushing, but I'm guilty, we all are, for letting him. I stood by all those times, just watching Will get pushed over the edge. I didn't *do* anything. And that is why I owe Will.

The siren screams to clear a path. I jump at the sound, my heart pounding in my throat as I move over and watch the ambulance roll by. As a kid, I always got a kick out of seeing ambulances with their sirens wailing and lights flashing. How dumb. Especially now that I know what they really mean.

Now that I know the person inside.

Shane watches the ambulance pull away. A strange look flickers across his face and then it's gone. He clenches his jaw and goes, "What an idiot. Leave it to Egghead to—"

"*Will!*" I snap. "His *name* is *Will.*"

Shane looks at me in surprise. For the first time, he doesn't have a comeback. Or if he does, he's keeping it to himself.

I head to the ski lodge, thinking about the hurt in Katie's eyes. And the look in Shane's. I wonder what it was. Fear maybe. Or guilt.

It's hard to say. I've never seen it on Shane before.

Katie

Over the next couple of weeks we wrote exams. We won the basketball tournament. We sold tickets to the Valentine's dance. We had fire drills and food fights. For students at St. Patrick's High School, life went on. But for one student, life was on hold.

Will closed his eyes on that hill, and he hadn't opened them since. He was in a coma.

I visited him nearly every day after the accident. He looked small, broken. Like a bird fallen out of its nest. The doctors had him hooked up to all kinds of machines and contraptions. His head was bandaged, his legs in slings and casts.

I always stopped in on my way home from Dad's room and just stood there, like an idiot, at the foot of Will's bed. I don't even know why I went. I never spoke to him. Will didn't even know I was there.

"Hey, girl," Maureen said, coming in to check the monitor. She turned a few knobs, checked his eyes, and wrote on the chart. Not that there was ever any news. It had been a few weeks and nothing changed but his bandages.

"You know, Katie," she clicked her pen and shoved it in her pocket. "Will is lucky to have a friend like you."

I tried to smile. If only she knew.

"Comatose patients wake up just like that," she snapped her fingers. "After months or even years—" She paused and looked away. "I mean . . . well, just keep coming."

I nodded.

"We're doing everything we can for him," she said. Nurse talk for: *it's up to Will now.* "And I'm no doctor," she walked around the bed and patted my shoulder on her way out. "But I always say it's what they have to come back for that makes all the difference."

I watched him sleep. *What has he got to come back to?* School? Not likely.

His family? Maybe. But I didn't think his dad was doing too well. I saw him in here last week, just as I was about to go in. He was slumped in the chair, head in his hands. "I can't do this, Melanie," he cried. "I can't. Not again."

It must have been so hard for Professor Reid. He was truly alone. His family lived in England. At least I had Granny. At least Dad was getting better—well, kind of. The professor's grief was still so raw, even now, two years later. I wanted to say something to give him hope, maybe share how Dad found strength after Mom died. Dad said I gave him a reason for living. *But if he lost that reason, too,* I thought looking at Will, bandaged and bruised. *What then?* I hesitated with my hand on the doorknob, ashamed to be witnessing something so private. Knowing the professor would not want to be seen this way, I stepped back into the hall and closed the door.

I stood at the foot of Will's bed. Maybe all he had to come back for was friends. A friend. Me. *I* was Will's closest friend. If you could call me a friend.

Who needs a friend like me?

"Will," I said softly. I walked to the bedside and put my hand over his. "I'm sorry. I let you down. I said things I never should have and never said something when it really mattered. But I just want you to know I . . . I care about you. Go, or come back. The choice is yours, Will." I squeezed his hand. "I just hope somehow you know you aren't alone."

Two days later, Will made his choice.

william james reid

Mom

You can't stay,
she said.
It's not time.

I'd thought I'd forgotten her face.
Seeing it now,
I remembered
what I always knew.

I love you, Will.

She never touched me.
But I could feel her.
Smell her.

Almost hold her.

She was only
one small step
away.

But it was a step
I wasn't ready
to take.

She smiled.

It made everything okay.
The light faded,
but I heard.
I knew.

I hope somehow you know you are not alone.

Devan

"'S'up Dev?" Shane says, shadowed by Brad. They slide onto the caf bench across from me. "We coulda used you last night. We were short a player."

I shrug, say something about my dad needing my help sanding something. I've been hanging around with him in his workshop a lot lately. Funny how I'd rather do that than be with Shane and Brad. I guess things are different now.

Or maybe I'm different.

No one ever mentions Will. But I can't get the guy out of my head. Or Katie.

I look over at her eating lunch all alone. She looks sad, smaller somehow. Like this whole thing has knocked the wind out of her. I think I know how she feels. I wish I could tell her. I wish I could just talk to her and see how Will's doing, how she's doing. I wonder what she'd do if I tried?

"Dev? You listening to me?" Shane says, blocking my view. He's frowning. Like it's a crime to ignore him.

"What? Yeah, sure. Whatever." I bite into my apple.

"So it's all set then." Shane smiles that smile. The one he wears when he gets a wicked idea. "I got the stuff in my locker. Meet you there in five minutes," he says and then heads out of the caf.

Brad gives me this look, like he knows something I don't, and grins.

Katie

"Is it true? Is he really awake?" Jenna scooted beside me on the empty bench. I chewed my tuna sandwich, trying to swallow it and the fact that Jenna was talking to me. I'd given up tagging along behind her and Isabella. They made it clear three was a crowd. I'd been spending my lunch hours reading, sitting all alone in a quiet corner in the stairwell. Besides, I wasn't interested in hearing the latest Mike report. Who cared if he got grounded, ate Lucky Charms this morning, or made the first string? Other than Jenna, of course.

"Yeah," I said. "He woke up a few days ago."

"Were you there? What was his first word?" She leaned in wide-eyed, way too interested for someone who hadn't asked about him once since the accident.

"*Mom*," I mumbled. "But I . . . uh . . . I wasn't there when he—"

Jenna stood. "*Mom*," she said, running back to her table where Isabella and the girls waited. "His first word was *Mom*." Everyone at the table stared at her, hungry for more information. Jenna spread it thick.

"Who?" Mike said, coming up from behind to hand Isabella a paper bag. "Here, dweeb. Ma put *your* lunch in my knapsack again."

Jenna's face glowed like a stoplight. "Uh—"

"Egghead," someone said.

"Oh yeah?" Mike looked at Jenna, then started to leave.

"Yeah," Jenna blurted. "But I bet he's got amnesia." Mike stopped. "Well, he must have anyway, 'cause he asked for his *mom*, right?" She leaned in and looked around as if she was trying not to let everyone hear. "And she died two years ago."

The girls gasped. "How?"

"Hit by a car," Jenna said, pausing for effect. "Will was with her. Saw the whole thing. It would have hit him, only she pushed him out of the way. She was in a coma for a few days too. Only she never woke up."

"Wow." Mike whispered, looking down at *Michael* scrawled in blue marker across the brown paper.

"Yeah." Jenna smiled, totally loving that she was having a conversation—a *conversation*—with Mike Montana. "That sure explains why he's like that, eh?"

I couldn't take another word or bite. "Yeah." I snapped, throwing my lunch in the garbage, "So what's *your* excuse?"

Truth was, I had no excuse either. Why was I acting like this? This wasn't me. No wonder everyone was avoiding me. But the question was, why was I avoiding Will?

He'd been awake for three days now and still I hadn't been to see him.

The day he woke up, Maureen dropped by Dad's room with the news. Granny and Dad cheered. Dad even put on his slippers and started wheeling his IV to the door to go and visit Will right then.

But I just couldn't. It was much easier to visit him when he was sleeping, when he never knew I was there. I still hadn't apologized to him. Maybe he didn't even want to see me. A jumble of feelings boiled in the middle of my chest and spilled down my face in hot tears. I couldn't stop.

"Maybe later, eh?" Granny had said. "Probably got his dad in there with him now, and doctors and such running tests." She looked at Dad over her glasses. "No need to be overwhelming the child."

We all knew she meant me.

Jenna's face went deep red. If there was a line, I had just crossed it. I had humiliated her in front of Saint Mike. I didn't wait for an answer. I just turned and walked out of the cafeteria as Mike's laughter and Jenna's glare followed me down the hall.

Devan

Shane pulls two large jars out of his locker. "I've been saving these for the right moment." He grins at Brad. "And it's now."

The jars are filled with worms. I'd wondered why Jackson said we were short. Shane's got this look in his eye like a kid at Christmas. He offers me a jar, but I shake my head. "I'm still eating my apple."

We walk down the hall. The teacher on hall duty isn't around, which is weird. Madame Latour usually patrols the place like a maximum-security prison.

Shane looks at me and, like he's reading my mind, goes, "Latour won't be back for a while—eh, Brad?"

Brad laughs. "I dropped some ex-lax in her coffee last class. She is, how you say, *beaucoup crappez.*"

I follow them to the end of the hall. Shane doesn't usually put so much thought into his plans. This premeditated stuff is taking him to a whole new level. I start to worry about what he's got in mind.

He stops at the landing and puts a finger to his lips as he unscrews the lid. So does Brad. "On the count of three," he whispers, pointing over the railing.

Why does he want to dump them down the stairs? It'll stink up two floors that way, but it just doesn't seem worth all the hype.

They put their jars on the ledge.

"One . . ."

I look over down the stairwell and notice someone sitting on the bottom step.

"Two . . ."

It's Katie.

"Thr—"

Before the word is out, I drive my shoulder into Shane and Brad, knocking them backwards. Both jars tip towards them, spilling worms everywhere. Shane jumps back just in time, but not Brad. He gets soaked in formaldehyde and slime as the glass jars crash around our feet.

"What the hell?!" Brad yells, looking at me like he's going to hit me. He slips on the worms and lands smack on his butt in the middle of them.

Shane just stares at me. I expect him to start razzing me about being a klutz. But he knows it wasn't an accident. Just like I know they targeted Katie on purpose, to test me.

"When are you two going to grow up?" I ask. And without waiting for an answer I walk away.

"You gonna let him away with that?" Brad asks. I can tell he's angry. Stinking like that, there's no way he'll get out of taking the rap for this one.

Shane doesn't answer, but his stare is burning a hole in my back. I don't care. They think I failed their stupid test.

But the way I see it, I passed.

Katie

After lunch, Isabella stopped with Jenna at her locker. They totally ignored me. Jenna just got her books and left, even though we were going to the same class. It was like I was invisible.

Too bad I wasn't. Maybe then Shane would leave me alone too.

Something was up. He was by himself, which was odd. Even more weird was how he kept staring at me the whole time. He was giving me the creeps. Those eyes, they were so intense, so angry. For a second, I thought maybe I *had* done something wrong.

I knelt and searched for my notebooks in the bottom of my locker. His eyes bored into my back.

Don't look at him. Don't look at him.

I rushed to get my stuff, spilling my pencil crayons around the floor. My hands shook as I reached for them.

The hall emptied. Kids headed to class. But not Shane. I knew he was still there. Watching. Waiting.

I grabbed what I could, slammed my locker shut, and got out of there, fast.

Devan

Seeing as he was soaked with formaldehyde, Brad gets busted for the worm jars and sent home early. I wonder what kind of story he'll tell his folks. Knowing his dad, he'll buy it. "Boys will be boys," he'll say and then tell Brad about all the trouble he used to get into in school.

I don't wait for Shane. I'm already at the bus stop when I see him come out of the school. I shuffle around in the snow trying to keep my feet warm, hoping the slush will wash off some of that formaldehyde stink.

Shane walks up and stands beside me. We don't say anything. What is there to say?

Finally he goes, "What's your problem, Dev?" Like I'm the one with a problem.

I don't answer. My feet are stinging from the cold. The bus is taking forever. I might as well just walk. "I'm outta here."

"Oh, what," he yells up the hill after me. "You think you're better than me, Dev?" He sounds almost desperate.

I keep walking.

"Well, you're not!" he shouts after me. "You're a loser, man. Nothing but a loser! Go ahead and walk away. You'll come crawling back. Some things never change!"

But he is wrong. Something has changed.

Me.

By the time I reach the top of the hill I know there's no way I'm walking home. Not in this weather. Not in these shoes. My feet are like ice. The only feeling left in my toes is a dull tingle. I cross the street and head for the hospital on the corner. My aunt works there. She is always telling me to stop by. Today seems as good a time as any to take her up on that offer of a ride.

"My shift is almost over," Aunt Maureen says with a big smile. She's so happy to see me I feel bad for waiting so long to drop by. "I'll be another fifteen minutes. Will that get you home in time for Em?"

I nod.

"Actually, Devan," she hands me a stack of library books. "I got these out for the patient in 242. Would you be a sweetie and bring them down?"

"Sure." I walk down the hall. "Visiting the library" probably isn't in her job description, but that's Aunt Maureen for you. She just has this way of giving you exactly what you need, sometimes even before you know you need it. I like that about her.

I find the room and knock.

"Come in," a voice calls from the other side. I open the door, surprised to see the room so bare. No cards, no flowers, no visitors. *Poor kid,* I think stepping in. *No wonder Aunt Maureen took this guy under her wing.*

"Just dropping off some stuff for—" my voice catches in my throat. It's him.

Will.

His leg is strung up. Tubes run in and out of his arms and nose. His broken body is covered in bandages and bruises. But it's his eyes that hit me hardest. He looks . . . scared.

I take a step back.

"Uh . . . here," I put the books on the table, "in case you want to read or something."

He doesn't move.

"So . . . uh . . . how are you doing?" I ask.

"Okay, I guess." He looks at me sideways. "Well, all things considered." He glances down at his leg.

"Looks like they got you pretty much cocooned there, don't they?"

"Yes. I'm a regular chrysalis, aren't I?" He relaxes a bit, settling back on his pillow. "Think I'll become a butterfly?"

"Who knows?" I say, staring hard at the floor. "Depends on if you think people can change."

He doesn't answer at first. But when I look up he is smiling at me.

"Yes," he says. "I think they can."

Aunt Maureen enters the room to fluff Will's pillow. She moves the book within reach.

"Thanks, Devan," Will says. "For the books, I mean. I really appreciate it."

"Oh, they're from—" I start to explain but Aunt Maureen squeezes my arm. Somehow, she knows it means more coming from me. "No problem." I start to leave and stop. "Next time I'll bring some on shedding cocoons."

"Yes," he laughs. "Yes. I'd like that very much."

william james reid

Trophallaxis

Foragers
store food
in their crop
to share with those
who are
hungry
yet unable to leave
the nest.

Nourishment,
given in the form of
liquid food,

or

library books.

Katie

I volunteered to clean out Mr. Jackson's aquarium. He wasn't going to get any more fish after somebody poisoned the last bunch. But I promised him we weren't all like that. I hoped that if someone showed interest and responsibility then he'd change his mind.

If nothing else, cleaning the tank kept me busy. It kept my mind off things. Mostly Jenna, Will, Shane, and Devan. And I figured that if I wasn't around, Shane might find some new hobby, other than me. Besides, I loved aquariums. I always wanted one. I'd milked the cleaning into a weeklong project.

"Katie, I appreciate you doing this," Mr. Jackson said. "I don't believe the tank ever looked so clean, even when I bought it." He scooped up a stack of assignments and opened the door. "Be sure to lock up when you leave."

I nodded and went back to scrubbing the tiny mermaid statue. *Maybe he'll let me be in charge of the tank for good,* I thought, hoping I could hide out in here for the rest of the year. I'd rather hang out with fish, anyway.

I smirked. *God, now I'm sounding like Will.*

I spent the whole lunch hour in there and I was just finishing up when I heard him.

"Well, if it isn't Katie." It was more of a threat than a greeting. I didn't have to look to know it was Shane. The statue fell from my hands. Brad leaned over and picked it up, looking at me as he snapped it in his fist.

"You're not supposed to be in here," I said, hoping they couldn't see the panic rippling up my back. My eyes darted between them.

"Not everyone does what they are *supposed* to do, Katie." Shane said, his voice eerily calm. "You were *supposed* to be in the lunchroom. Brad and I are *supposed* to raid the fetal pig jars. But things don't always go the way you want. You just make the best of it—eh, Brad?"

Brad chuckled.

"I have to go," I said, inching towards the door. Brad stepped out, blocking the way.

Shane looked me over and sneered. "I don't know what Devan sees in you."

My face flushed at Devan's name. "I have to go—" The words stuck in my dry mouth.

Shane stepped forward, backing me up against the tank. There was no escape, now. I was trapped. Suddenly I understood. I saw how it must have been for Will all those months. *Stand up to him. Don't let him push you around. Don't give him power over you.* Those "strategies" echoed hollow and empty in my head. It was a lot easier to give that advice than to take it.

I swallowed and looked Shane right in the face. "You don't scare me, Shane," I said, trying to keep my voice from wobbling as much as my legs. I gripped the table behind me. "I am not afraid of you."

"Well, you should be," he said in a low whisper. "You *should* be."

Devan

I head to the lab early. My assignment's overdue, but maybe I can sneak it into the pile on his desk. At least, I hope so. Luckily it's Potluck Tuesday. Jackson never gets out of the teacher's lounge on time while there's a Crock-Pot cooking, so I've got a few minutes.

I enter the lab, surprised to see Shane. Something's up. *Is he scamming worms? Trashing the aquarium again?*

Then I see Katie. Shane's got her cornered over by the fish tank. She's sheet white and her eyes are wicked huge. She's scared, real scared.

My first instinct is to jump in there and pound the crap out of Shane for scaring her like that. But instead, I walk to Jackson's desk beside him and drop my assignment.

"Picking on girls now, Shane?" I say, like I'm just making conversation.

Shane's ears go red. He turns to face me. "What did you say?"

"He said 'Picking on—'" Brad echoes.

"You heard me," I say real quiet, meeting Shane stare for stare. He can't pull that one on me. I know his tricks. "Leave her alone."

Shane snatches Katie's wrist as she tries to get by again. His eyes never leave mine. "You gonna make me?"

My jaw clenches. I hope he's not saying what I think he is. He knows I can kick his butt. If I have to.

The bell rings and the door clicks open. The class comes in, but I know Jackson won't be here for a little while longer. Sensing a fight, everyone gathers around us for a ringside seat.

"C'mon, Dev," Shane says, like we're all buddy-buddy. "Lighten up, man. We're just joking is all."

"It's not funny."

"Well, *we* think it is," Shane looks around the crowd. "Don't we?"

Nobody speaks.

He singles out a few with his stare, but they look away, shuffle their feet, or look at Katie wriggling in his grip, still trying to break free. Her wrist is red from all the wrenching and twisting. Shane glares at her, then me. He still doesn't get it.

"Only trash would hurt a girl . . . right?" I say, throwing his own words back at him. "Or are you taking after Riley, Shane?"

I can see the realization hit him. He reels like I just punched him in the gut, his eyes wide with shock as he stares at the truth. For a moment, he looks like he might even cry. Then his anger takes over, burning away everything else, till all he sees is red.

"Shut up!!" He lets go of her wrist and shoves me hard into the desk. "Just shut your freaking mouth! I'm *nothing* like him!"

Katie disappears into the crowd. But Shane doesn't care. This isn't about her anymore.

It's not even about me.

It's about him.

Katie

Devan hit the desk hard, landing on his back. Books and papers went flying everywhere as Shane jumped on top of him. Mr. Jackson's glass barometer hit the floor and exploded into a million pieces. Shane pounded his fists into Devan's sides, but Devan's bent arms blocked some of the blows. I'd never seen Shane so out of control.

"Get him! Get him, Shane!" Brad cheered.

Devan got a knee up and pushed Shane off. But Shane was right back on him as he rolled off the desk. Grabbing handfuls of shirt, they wrestled each other across the front of the room. Glass crunched under their feet.

Shane tried to get a few punches over Devan's thick arms, catching him on the cheek, and the jaw. But Devan drove forward, pushing Shane against the wall, and lifting him by fistfuls of his collar.

"Say you're sorry," Devan grunted through clenched teeth.

Shane squirmed and kicked.

"Say . . . you're . . . sorry!" Devan said again.

"Screw you!" Shane spat on him.

There was no way in heck Shane was going to apologize, ever. But Devan wasn't giving up. And I knew it wasn't about just me anymore. It was bigger than that. Bigger than what Shane did to Will even. It was like Devan wanted to hear Shane take responsibility for something, *anything*, even if he had to squeeze it out of him.

"Geez, Shane! Say you're freakin' sorry!" Devan said.

Suddenly Brad appeared out of nowhere with Jackson's yardstick. He swung it like a bat, breaking it across Devan's back. Devan arched in pain, dropping Shane.

A mix of blood, sweat, and spit ran down Devan's face as he gasped for breath. Brad stood over him waving the broken ruler.

"Who's sorry now, loser?" Brad asked with a wicked grin.

"You are," Mr. Jackson said, entering the classroom and staring at the three of them.

Devan

Jackson marches us right to Spence's office. Spence meets with Jackson for a few minutes, then calls us in one by one, starting with Brad.

Shane and I sit in the waiting room, but his eyes never leave the carpet. He never says a word. He must be thinking about all that has happened. How far he has gone. After a few minutes, Spence's door opens and Brad comes out.

"Mr. Duran," Spence calls. Shane goes in next. Spence's mumble starts like a hive of bees.

"So?" I ask Brad. "What'd he say?"

"Well, because I *used a weapon* and the fact that I'd already got busted for that worm thing, Spence gave me a two-week suspension and a warning. If I step a foot out of line—I'm outta here. Whatever." He shrugs like it's no biggie and leaves. Knowing Brad, he'll take that as a challenge. His dad's been itching to send him to that military school anyway. Said that's where he learned how to be a real man.

Shane's voice rises and falls, breaking the silence of the waiting room. A couple of times I hear Spence's low mumble. After a good half hour, the door clicks open and there's Shane, wiping his nose on his sleeve. *Has he been crying?* Spence walks him to the office door and puts his hand on his shoulder. "We covered a lot of ground today. Go home, and I'll see you for our meeting tomorrow, son."

"Okay, sir." Shane says. He looks smaller, somehow. Like some of the air has been let out of him. I almost feel sorry for him. He heads for the hall, then stops and turns. "Thanks, Mr. Spence."

What the heck did Spence say in there? I wonder. He hadn't talked much at all, mostly just listening. Was that what Shane really needed?

"Mr. Mitchell?"

I get up and follow Spence into his office. He motions for me to sit in one of the chairs in front of his big desk. He sits in the other.

"Why don't you tell me what happened, son," he says. So I do. Spence listens carefully as though he hadn't already heard this story three times before.

"Well, it sounds like you were defending Katie. You never threw a punch. It was two against one and Brad hit you from behind. Is that right?"

I nod. *Geez, when you put it like that, I sound like some kinda hero.*

"But," he continues, "the fact is you were fighting and you *did* some damage to Mr. Jackson's desk and classroom. Although your intentions are noble, Devan, there are always consequences for your actions."

In the end, he gives me a two-day suspension. It sounds fair to me. I only hope it sounds as fair to Mom and Dad.

I manage to change my shirt before Mom and Dad get home, but there's no changing my face. It's pretty messed up. All cut, scabbed, and bruised. Mom starts crying when she sees me.

"Oh, sweetie, have a seat and let me get you a snack." She fusses in the kitchen and then hands me a wicked huge bowl of chocolate mint ice cream. Like it will make my back feel any better. Funny enough, it does. Weird how moms know that, eh?

"Okay, Dev. What's the deal? What happened?" Dad asks. Mom joins us at the kitchen table and I spill the whole story; about Shane and Brad, about Will—I even tell them about Katie.

Mom gets all weepy again over my "emotional scars" from being rejected by my friends and all. But pity is good, considering the next thing I have to tell them is that I'm suspended for a few days. Surprisingly, they're both pretty understanding.

"You can't change other people, Devan. Not Shane or Brad or anyone else for that matter." Dad says. "The only person you can change is yourself. And that takes work." He pats my shoulder. "Since you've got some time on your hands, I suggest you spend it considering what things *you* need to work on."

I lick the ice cream off the back of the spoon and head downstairs to the workshop.

A few days off are just what I need to get started on my apology.

Katie

"And what did Mr. Spence say?" Dad asked. I sat on the edge of his bed filling him in on what had happened that day.

"I don't know what he said, but the guys all got suspensions."

"Devan too?"

I nodded.

"Are you nervous about seeing Shane again?"

For some reason, I wasn't. Mr. Spence knew, now. Thanks to Devan, everyone saw Shane for what he was—just another kid. An angry kid, but still just a kid. I still couldn't believe Devan did that . . . for me.

"Well, it's great to know there are good people out there who do the right thing," Dad said.

"Speaking of the right thing," I pushed myself out of the chair and walked to the door. "I have something I've been meaning to do for a long time."

Dad smiled. He knew where I was going. Will's room.

We weren't going to be in the hospital many more days. Dad's cancer was in remission. This morning the doctors told him he'd be going home in a day or two. But I'd still come and visit Will. If he'd have me.

I knocked on the door to room 242, relieved and kind of nervous to finally be getting this off my chest. No one answered, so I let myself in. Will deserved to know that I was sorry, that I cared about him as a friend and nothing was going to stop me from telling him that now.

The room was empty. The bed, stripped. *Oh God!*

I ran down the hall to the nurse's station. "Maureen! Will's bed is empty—he's not in his room!" Panic rose in my voice. An empty bed usually meant one thing for a patient who was not ready to be discharged.

"Katie," Maureen waved her hands to calm me down, "Honey, it's okay. He's okay. His dad got a job transfer."

"What?"

"They're moving, to his hometown university. I thought you knew."

I shook my head. "When?"

"They left two days ago," she put her hand on my shoulder, "for England."

"Did he leave a note or anything?" I asked. She shook her head. Even after all that had happened, I couldn't believe he'd just left without saying good-bye. But maybe I deserved it, after what I did to him.

I never told him, not while he was awake anyway. I never apologized. I never let him know how much our friendship really meant to me, or that someone cared.

And now he would never know.

Devan

"Well now, it's great to meet you, Devan," she hands me a glass of lemonade. "Katie's told me all about you."

I can't believe I'm here, in Katie's house. I can't believe she told her grandmother about me. What *did* she tell her? I clear my throat and shift on the couch, holding the glass in both hands so it won't shake.

Her grandmother sits in the chair across from me and smiles.

Whatever Katie told her, I guess it wasn't all bad. I mean, even with my cuts and bruises, her grandmother isn't looking at me like I'm some kind of thug.

"They should be here any minute," she says looking at her watch and smiling. "Her father's coming home from the hospital today. The cancer is in remission."

I didn't even know her dad was sick. "Maybe I should just come some other time. I don't want to be in the way—"

A car door slams.

"Oh, there they are now." She stands up and pats my arm. "Katie will be glad to see you."

Only I'm not so sure. I feel like I might puke.

"I'm hooo-oome!" a man's voice calls as he comes in the living room. He gives Katie's grandmother a hug and then looks at me.

"John, this is Devan. Katie's friend," her grandmother says.

I stand up, spilling lemonade. "Oh, I . . . uh—"

"Nice to finally meet you, Devan," he puts out his hand. I wipe mine on my pants and shake hands, hoping he thinks it's wet from lemonade and not clammy from nerves.

Then she walks in the room. She sees me. Her mouth drops open and her cheeks go all red, like she can't believe I'm here. I can't tell how she's feeling, other than shocked. To be honest, I'm a little shocked I'm here myself.

I had practiced what I wanted to say a million times. It was totally cool. But all I get out is, "Hey."

"Why don't you let me take that for you?" her grandmother says. My glass is half empty and I haven't even taken a sip. I'm standing there, still spilling it as I look at Katie.

"Oh, right." I give it to her and shove my hands in my pockets. "Sorry about that."

"Come on now, John," her grandmother says leading him out of the room. "I'll help you unpack."

The door clicks behind them, leaving Katie and me still standing in the middle of the room.

I take a deep breath. "So . . . uh . . . how are you?"

Katie

How am I?

Good question. The last few days had been such a roller-coaster. I hardly had a moment to think: Shane's attack, Dad's good news, Will leaving, and now Devan here. *Devan Mitchell,* standing in my living room.

What's he doing here?

"I'm good," I finally said. My heart thudded as I looked up at him. I'd never noticed his eyes were so blue. "How are *you*? Wow, your face looks so sore."

"Nah," he shrugged, and looked at me for a moment. Neither of us said anything. Then he took a deep breath. "Listen, Katie, I've been meaning to tell you for a long time, and well, it's just that I . . ." he stared at his feet. "I know you think I trashed your science fair project, but it wasn't me."

It was good to know that for sure. "Who did it?" I asked, like I didn't already know. "Shane?"

He nodded. "But I still owe you an apology." He looked me in the eyes. "I was there. I saw Shane do it and I should've done something to stop him. I should've saved your farm, Katie. But I didn't and . . . I'm sorry."

I didn't know what to say. I could tell it took a lot for him to come here and tell me that. Before I could answer, he picked up a big package wrapped in brown paper and handed it to me.

"Here."

I sat on the couch and opened it.

"I know it's not as good or as big as your real one," he said shifting foot to foot, "but, well, I . . . uh . . . I made it for you."

It was an ant farm. The wood framing the glass was shaped like a barn and painted bright red. It even had barn doors that opened and closed on either side. And a little sign hung from the top that read, "Brayside Farm." My eyes filled with tears.

He noticed me crying. "You're right," he said reaching to take it back. "It's stupid. I shouldn't have—"

I put my hand on his. "Thank you, Devan," I smiled. "It's perfect."

We set it on the table. He seemed relieved as he sat beside me on the couch. "Will gave me the basic design, but I added all that other stuff myself."

"Who?" I asked.

"Will," he said. "I've been visiting him the last few weeks, you know, taking him books and stuff."

"*You've* been visiting *Will*?" I couldn't hide the shock in my voice and the shame. I should have been visiting too. "I can't believe he's gone. I never even said good-bye."

"Oh, yeah, here," Devan handed me an envelope. "He asked me to give you this."

The envelope had *Katie* scrawled across the front in Will's handwriting.

I opened it up. There was a poem inside:

Metamorphosis

What if a queen
remained
an egg?

Afraid of change.

Unwilling to grow.

Cocooned in fear,
how many lives
would she leave untouched?

Sometimes it hurts
to grow,

to rebuild paths,

or follow those
that lead to
new colonies.

But we do it, anyway.

"Go to the ant.
Consider its ways
and be wise."

Katie, you are a queen.

Trust your instincts.

For in your heart
you know
each end
is really
just

a new beginning.

Love,
Will

Devan

I think she really likes the farm. What a relief! I was so freaked out about giving it to her. Now I'm so glad I did.

I have to email Will as soon as I get home and let him know how much she loved it. He said she would. I kind of wondered if it was something he wanted to give her, but I never asked. Maybe 'cause I didn't really want to know.

"Wait a second," Katie says. "There's something else in here." She pulls out a smaller envelope stuffed inside the big one. "It's got your name on it."

I rip the side of the envelope and pull out a slip of paper.

"What is it?" Katie asks, leaning in as I flip it over.

It's the Mexicasa gift certificate.

"I could, I mean, we could . . ." I trip over my words again. "If you want to—"

Katie puts her hand on my arm and smiles. "I'd like that."

I smile too. It hurts my cheek, but I just can't stop.

This was your first published novel, released in 2008. What led to your wanting to tell this story?

In 2003, I had the chance to take a writing class offered by the talented Jerry Spinelli. In it, he shared the best advice I've ever received about writing, and I've followed that advice in every novel since: "Start with an emotionally charged memory." That day, I wrote a short scene about my memories of being bystander to bullying when I was in Grade 7. Little did I know that I was actually beginning Katie's voice in *Egghead*.

A few chapters into the first draft, I realized I had to tell this story from more than one point of view. I knew what it was like to be the friend of the victim, to ask: *Do I have the courage to stand up for my friend?* But I wondered what would it have been like to be friends with the bully, to ask: *Do I have the courage to stand up to my friend?*

Egghead asks the question every bystander thinks: *How long will I stand by?*

Why do you think this book has been so successful with young readers—as well as with teachers and parents?
Over the past decade since *Egghead* was released, I've had such incredible feedback from readers. Kids relate to the characters and their problems. They see themselves or someone they know in Shane, Devan, Katie, or Will. I've been so touched to hear how this story has connected with the stories of their real lives—to know it has inspired them to speak up against bullying, to ask for help, or to know they are not alone.

Readers are usually drawn into a story through the character with whom they most relate. *Egghead's* multiple points of view offers multiple ways in. For example, someone who can't relate to Katie might still be drawn in by Will or Devan's voice. But what I love most about multiple points of view is that it shows me what life is like for someone different than me. Ultimately, that strengthens empathy.

Teachers and parents have shared that this is a novel their kids can't put down. It's the story that has kids begging to read "just one more chapter!" As a parent and teacher, I know how rare and wonderful it is when your kids are engaged and excited about reading. Inspired by popular writers like Dan Brown, I used fast-paced, short chapters that ended with cliffhangers.

But I think *Egghead's* greatest appeal is its heart. It gets kids thinking, relating, and empathizing. It gets kids talking.

You made a point of showing that the bully in this story has his own issues to deal with. Why was that important to you?

Every person has a story. We might never know what they are going through or what they are dealing with if they don't tell us, but it still affects the way they act. Shane doesn't have a voice in the book. Because of that, we aren't sure exactly what is going on inside of him or why he is so mean. As in real life, we might judge him harshly based on his actions, words, and attitudes. But through his friend Devan's eyes, we see clues of what might be happening in Shane's life. Often the people who hurt others are hurt themselves. If we remember that we are more likely to offer compassion rather than judgement.

It is sometimes said that if bystanders took action, bullies would not pose such a threat to their victims. Why do you think this is true?

Back in the 80's, we weren't taught about bullying awareness. I didn't even realize I was a bystander. I was a shy, scrawny girl—it never even crossed my mind that I had any power. But the truth is: I did have power. So do you. So does every bystander. However the bullying happens—whether it's physical, verbal, or even online—when we stand by and just watch, it's like we are saying: "I'm okay with this." We are actually fueling the bully's power. But when we have the courage to speak up and let people know, "This isn't okay!" we invite others to do the same.

Every bystander has a choice: you can empower the bully or empower one another. What would you choose?

At the end of the story, Katie finds out that Will and his father have moved away and she will not see him again. Do you think it would have been possible for Will to have returned to this school after recovering from such a serious injury?

Yes, I do. Will had developed a good relationship with Devan and things had changed with Shane. I think facing and overcoming his worst fear made Will stronger in the end. People who related with Will the most have let me know that they were disappointed by the ending. They wanted Will to finally confront and defeat Shane but, honestly, that wouldn't be Will's way. I don't think he would have told off Shane or done something to hurt him in revenge. Will is the kind of guy who forgives and befriends Devan. He's the kind of guy who gives the girl he most admires the chance to date the guy she likes, even if it's not him. That's who Will is—a person of great character and strength.

I had Will move away in the end, because my friend who was bullied moved away. I also know that for many kids who are bullied, the right choice is to start fresh at a new school.

In this new edition of the book, what made you decide to change some of the language used by the characters — words like fag, retard, and spaz?

When I was a teenager and even up until shortly after *Egghead* was released, these kinds of words were used in everyday conversation. We thought it was okay because we were "just joking." But as people, particularly young people, became more aware of how those words affected others, they decided to stop using them. They helped others realize how offensive such offhand comments were. Surprisingly, I've had mixed responses about taking out these words. Some teachers are glad because, like me, they used to edit those words out as they read the book aloud. Other people felt the words not only helped define characters like Shane—but also led to some great teachable moments and conversations when their students reacted to Shane's choice of words.

All in all, it's taught me that words are powerful—but that in the end, we control that power.

When you meet young people who have read the book, what kinds of things do they tell you about their experiences with bullying?
Over the years, so many young readers have shared how profoundly *Egghead* affected them. It helped bystanders see their power and potential to make a difference. It encouraged kids like Will to know they were not alone—and many wrote to tell me that because of the story, they actually told a friend, teacher, or parent about their own struggles. Kids like Devan wrote to tell me about the challenges of having a friend who made bad choices and how Devan inspired them to stand up for what they believed.

But perhaps the most moving letters of all were the ones I got from kids like Shane: kids who were mistreated; kids whose home lives were unstable or violent; kids who hadn't realized why the other kids disliked them but who now saw the truth because of Shane's story. "I hadn't realized I was a bully," one kid wrote. "But now I do and I'm going to try not to be like that anymore."

What do teachers tell you about their use of the novel, in terms of better understanding of the effects of bullying?
Bullying awareness is widespread now—and that is wonderful! We see things like pink shirt days, bullying prevention programs, and Bullying Awareness Week. There are lots of great resources for teaching our students the facts about bullying.

But teachers also know that one of the most powerful ways to engage our kids is through story. Story takes us on a journey and even though we are living vicariously through the characters, we are experiencing what they do. We feel what they feel. Story changes us. Over the years, countless teachers have shared with me how this novel sparked profound class discussions, debates, and, above all, positive changes. Using *Egghead* gives their students a safe way to experience, analyze, and discuss real life issues and to learn from the struggles of fictional characters.

Even though other books you have written have won major awards and been praised by reviewers, *Egghead* could be seen as your most successful novel and is still selling well after more than ten years. Why do you think that is so?
Maybe it's the emotional charge. Maybe it's the fast pace or multiple voices. Maybe it's because teachers and parents support the message or because readers relate to the characters. I think my writing keeps improving, I hope it does, but *Egghead* continues to resonate with people in ways that amaze me and I'm so thankful for that.

You have written many more books in the years since *Egghead* came out. What have you learned about your craft as a writer during those years? How has being a published author changed your life, if at all?

Egghead took me five years to write, because I had no idea how to write a novel. *Where do you start? Where does it end? What do I put in this next chapter?* I think the greatest thing I've learned about the craft is to really know my characters. In my experience, it prevents writer's block. When I know a character like I would a close friend, I already know what they'll say or do in a certain situation. Their desires and weaknesses create the conflict. Their continuous attempts to succeed drive the plot. I've learned and taught that there's no "right way" to write a story. But a story that is character-driven seems to work best for me. They are the stories I love to read, so it's not surprising they are the stories I love to write.

It is a wild and wonderful thing to have a book published, to have people peek inside my head and heart, to have them care as deeply about my characters as I do—because those characters are a part of me. Thanks to all those readers for making them a part of you, too.

What advice do you have for young people who want to write their own stories?

I could tell my twenty-six Writer's Craft students to write about the *Titanic* and I would get twenty-six completely different stories. Sure—some facts might be the same (hello iceberg, goodbye ship), but each story would be unique because each student is unique.

Only you have your unique personality and talents, your history, or your place in your family. You have a certain point of view, a specific sense of humor, and a well-stocked imagination. There is only one you!

That means: Only you can write *your* story. So my advice would be to follow Jerry Spinelli's advice: Start with an "emotionally charged memory." Start there and trust your voice. Write about what moves you in a way that interests you—and you can bet that it will move and interest your readers too.

Thank you, Caroline, for all your insights and for this powerful story.

Caroline Pignat is an award-winning author of highly acclaimed novels for young adults. *Egghead* is her first novel. A short story she wrote in Grade 11 inspired her next novel *Greener Grass*, winner of the 2009 Governor General's Literary Award. *The Gospel Truth*, a novel in poetry, won her a second Governor General's Literary Award in 2015. Caroline lives, writes, and teaches in Ottawa.